"You need to tell the sheriff *everything* that happened..."

Tires squealed around the corner, and a dark sedan with tinted windows approached at a high speed. Noah quickly ushered Ruthie and the boys away from the road. The car's front tire came up on the sidewalk.

Ruthie screamed and shoved the boys farther from the car. Noah turned as it raced past.

Ruthie grabbed Noah's hand. "If you had not moved us away from the curb, I fear what would have happened." Tears filled her eyes.

He wrapped his arm around her shoulder and then pulled the boys into his embrace, as well. "The car's gone, and we're all okay."

"But—"

He nodded to her, knowing there was a reason the car had jumped the curb, and it wasn't because the driver was going too fast. He was sure the guy was the same man who had come after Ruthie.

Noah glanced in the direction the car had gone. The guy who wanted Ruthie's property was becoming unhinged.

One thing was certain: Ruthie and the boys were in his crosshairs.

Debby Giusti is an award-winning Christian author who met and married her military husband at Fort Knox, Kentucky. Together they traveled the world, raised three wonderful children and have now settled in Atlanta, Georgia, where Debby spins tales of mystery and suspense that touch the heart and soul. Visit Debby online at debbygiusti.com, blog with her at seekerville.blogspot.com and craftieladiesofromance.blogspot.com, and email her at Debby@DebbyGiusti.com.

Books by Debby Giusti

Love Inspired Suspense

Her Forgotten Amish Past
Dangerous Amish Inheritance

Amish Witness Protection

Amish Safe House

Amish Protectors

Amish Refuge
Undercover Amish
Amish Rescue
Amish Christmas Secrets

Visit the Author Profile page at Harlequin.com for more titles.

DANGEROUS AMISH INHERITANCE

DEBBY GIUSTI

LOVE INSPIRED SUSPENSE

INSPIRATIONAL ROMANCE

LOVE INSPIRED® SUSPENSE
INSPIRATIONAL ROMANCE

ISBN-13: 978-1-335-40273-8

Dangerous Amish Inheritance

Recycling programs
for this product may
not exist in your area.

Love Inspired
22 Adelaide St. West, 40th Floor
Toronto, Ontario M5H 4E3, Canada
www.Harlequin.com

Printed in U.S.A.

Deliver me out of the mire, and let me not sink:
let me be delivered from them that hate me,
and out of the deep waters.
Let not the waterflood overflow me,
neither let the deep swallow me up,
and let not the pit shut her mouth upon me.
Hear me, O Lord; for thy lovingkindness is good:
turn unto me according to the multitude of
thy tender mercies.
—*Psalm* 69:14-16

In memory of
Becky Martin
February 28, 1950–April 16, 2019

A beautiful sister in Christ!
I miss you, dear friend.

ONE

Ruthie Eicher awoke with a start. She blinked in the darkness, hearing the patter of March rain on the tin roof, and touched the opposite side of the double bed, where her husband had slept. Two months since the tragic accident and she was not yet used to his absence.

Finding the far side of the bed empty and the sheets cold, she dropped her feet to the floor, tied the flannel robe around her waist and hurried into the hallway. Sorrow twisted her heart as she peered into her father's room, unoccupied since the buggy crash that had killed her husband and claimed her *datt*'s life, as well. Had her mother been alive she would have said it was *Gott*'s will, although Ruthie placed the blame on her husband's failure to approach the intersection with caution. According to the sheriff's report, the *Englischer*'s car had the right of way, which her husband failed to acknowledge.

Ruthie hurried to the children's room. Even without lighting the oil lamp, she knew from the steady draw of their breaths that nine-year-old Simon and six-year-old Andrew were sound asleep.

Danki, Gott. She lifted up a prayer of thanks for her two wonderful sons, one blond, one brunette, both so different yet so loved. After adjusting the coverings around the boys' shoulders, she peered from their window and gazed out at the farm that was falling into disrepair.

Movement near the outbuildings caught her eye. She

held her breath and stared for a long moment, unsure of what she had seen.

Narrowing her gaze, she leaned forward, and her heart raced as a flame licked the air.

She shook Simon. "The woodpile. On fire. I need help."

He rubbed his eyes.

"Hurry, Simon."

Leaving him to crawl from bed, she raced downstairs, almost tripping, her heart pounding as she knew all too well how quickly the fire could spread. She ran through the kitchen, grabbed the back doorknob and groaned as her fingers struggled with the lock.

"No!" She moaned and coaxed her fumbling hands to work. The lock disengaged. She threw open the door and ran across the porch and down the steps.

Cold Georgia mountain air swirled around her, along with the acrid smell of smoke. Rain dampened her hair and robe. She raced to the pump, grabbed a nearby bucket and filled it, then scrambled to the woodpile and hurled the water onto the flames. The fire hissed as if taunting her efforts to quell the blaze. Returning to the pump, she filled another bucket, then another.

A noise sounded behind her. She glanced over her shoulder, expecting Simon. Instead she saw a large, darkly dressed figure. Something struck the side of her head. She gasped with pain, dropped the bucket and stumbled toward the house.

He grabbed her shoulder and threw her to the ground. She cried, struggled to her knees and started to crawl away. He kicked her side. She groaned and tried to stand. He tangled his fingers through her hair and pulled her to her feet.

She turned, her arms flailing, and made out only a shadowed form of a man. A lady's stocking distorted his face. A knit cap covered his hair. She dug her fingernails into his neck.

He twirled her around and yanked her arm up behind her back. Pain, like white lightning, exploded along her spine. She reared back to ease the pressure.

The man's lips touched her ear. "Didn't you read my notes? You don't belong here." His rancid breath soured the air. "Leave before something happens to you and your children."

Her heart stuttered.

He threw her to the wet ground and kicked her again. Air whizzed from her lungs. She gasped, unable to breathe.

The back door creaked open, and Simon stood in the doorway, eyes wide. *"Mamm?"*

"Stay…inside." Ruthie glanced at the now smoldering logs. She was relieved by the dying fire, and even more grateful that the man had disappeared.

Andrew pushed past his older brother and grabbed the rope to the dinner bell that hung on the back porch. His face twisted with determination as he tugged on the heavy hemp. The peel of the bell sounded in the night.

Simon ran to where she was lying and fell to his knees. *"Mamm*, do not die. Do not die like *Datt."*

She wanted to reassure both boys, but all she could think of was that no one would answer their call for help.

Noah Schlabach stepped from his father's house and inhaled the smoke that hung heavy in the air. The chilling clang of a dinner bell pierced the silence. At this time of night, it signaled danger and need. The closest neighboring farm on Amish Mountain belonged to Eli Plank. Ten years ago, the crusty old codger had a bad heart and a cranky disposition. Doubting Eli's condition had improved, Noah climbed behind the wheel of his Ford pickup, flicked on the lights and headed along the dirt road that led to the bridge, which he hoped was still standing. Rain had fallen steadily since he had returned to the area twenty-four hours ago and had swelled the narrow river. There was a safer bridge closer to town, but the detour would delay his response to the bell's clamant call.

He'd last crossed the river the night he had begged Eli's daughter, Ruthie, to run away with him. Leaving her ten years ago had been the hardest thing he'd ever done, next to burying his brother, Seth, and his family. Coming back to sell their father's house was closure to the past and all its pain. If only he could rid himself of the guilt so he could embrace life again. But then, he didn't deserve happiness. Nor did he expect to find it.

The wind howled, bending the pines and pushing against the truck with a powerful force. He gripped the steering wheel as he neared the rickety bridge. The guard railings bowed in the wind. A board broke loose, fell into the water and floated downstream toward the town of Willkommen.

Had he remained Amish, Noah would have offered a prayer for his own safe passage over the aged structure, but if God hadn't answered Noah's prayers for his brother, He wouldn't answer his prayer tonight. Better to remain silent than to face God's rejection again.

The moon broke through the clouds and reflected off the churning river below. Glancing higher up the mountain, he spied the cascading waterfall. The early spring rains had been merciless, which added to the surge of water flowing down the mountain.

He eased the truck across the bridge and accelerated on the other side. The Plank farmhouse sat at the upper tip of the valley, not more than fifty yards from the riverbank. Too close to the water, but then Mr. Plank had never made good decisions about the way he managed his farm, or how he parented Ruthie after her mother's death.

A small boy with blond hair, not more than five or six, stood on the porch, ringing the dinner bell. Noah braked to a stop and lunged from the truck. A fire smoldered in the woodpile. Smoke trailed upward from what appeared to be a contained burn.

Turning, his heart sped up.

An older boy was kneeling over a woman who was lying facedown in the red Georgia clay. Noah recognized the dark hair and frail form.

Ruthie!

"Mamm," the child whimpered as Noah neared. "Help her," the boy pleaded. "Help my *mamm.*"

Noah touched her slender neck, searched for a pulse and let out a relieved breath when he felt a faint but steady beat.

She moaned and tried to turn over. Her neck and spine seemed uninjured, yet her eyes remained closed. Feeling her arms, he checked for breaks, then did the same to her legs and feet before he gently lifted her into his arms.

"Let's take your *mamm* inside."

The older boy hurried to the porch, where his younger brother held on to the bell rope as if his hands were glued in place.

"It's okay," Noah assured the shivering younger child. "Come inside and get warm."

Following the boys into the house, he asked, "Where's your mother's bedroom?"

"On the second floor." The older boy locked the kitchen door behind them, then led the way up the stairs.

Peering around the starkly furnished Amish home, Noah expected to see Eli. "Is your grandfather asleep?" he asked.

"*Dawdy* died two months ago," the young one said.

"And your father?"

"He died in the same buggy accident."

Noah's gut tightened. "There are just you two boys?"

They nodded.

"And *Mamm*," the younger one answered. His fingers latched onto his mother's arm, which was hanging limp. Tears welled in his eyes.

"She's going to be okay." Although Noah wanted to reassure the child, he wasn't sure of any such thing. Ruthie had been used as a punching bag. Internal injuries could be deceptive and hard to diagnose. She needed a doctor, but knowing the Amish way was to treat first and use medical care as a last option, he would assess her injuries before he talked about taking her to the hospital in Willkommen.

The boys led him into a small bedroom. The covers on the bed had been thrown back. Ruthie's slippers sat on the floor. Carefully, he removed her muddy robe and laid her on the bed.

"*Datt* said we deserved it whenever we were hurt," the little one whispered. "But *Mamm* did not deserve to be beaten. Ever."

Had she been beaten before? "Did either of you see the person who hurt your *mamm*?"

Both boys shook their heads.

Noah touched her cheek. "Ruthie?"

She moaned.

"Talk to her, boys."

"*Mamm*, look at me. It's Andrew." The youngest one leaned over his mother and kissed her cheek.

Noah's heart tightened.

The other boy, his face shadowed, touched her hair. "Open your eyes, *Mamm*. Simon wants to see your blue eyes."

Andrew started to cry.

Noah put his arm around the young child and drew him close. "Shhh," he soothed.

The older boy turned to the nightstand. He struck a match and lit the oil lamp.

With the sudden burst of light, Ruthie's eyes blinked open. She stared at Noah, her brow furrowed with puzzlement.

"Your boys are safe," he assured her.

"Andrew?" She tried to raise her head.

"Here I am, *Mamm*."

"And Simon?" Slowly, she turned to look at her oldest child.

Noah followed her gaze, seeing the boy more clearly in the lamplight. Tall and lean, he had a shock of brown hair about the same shade as Noah's. Dark eyes, a strong nose and square jaw. One eyebrow arched slightly higher than the other. His lips were full. He offered his mother a weak smile, revealing dimples on each cheek.

Noah's gut tightened. He raised his hand to his own face. The realization hit him hard as he stared at the boy who looked surprisingly like him.

"Why did you come back, Noah?" Ruthie asked, her tone bitter as she turned to stare at him. "You left once—why did you return to Amish Mountain?"

Before seeing Simon in the light, he would have told her he was here to sell his deceased father's house and farm. Now he realized something other than his father's passing had brought him back to the mountain. Was it Divine Providence? Whether God was involved, he would never know, but one thing was certain—Noah had been led back to Amish Mountain to find his son.

TWO

Noah!

Ruthie pushed aside the dream that troubled her slumber and opened her eyes to the light streaming through her bedroom window. Her head pounded with confusion as she struggled to remember everything that had happened last night. Mentally, she flipped through a number of details until she stopped at the fire and the man who had attacked her.

His words made her stomach roil. *You don't belong here. Leave before something happens to you and your children.*

Remembering the two notes with similar warnings that had been shoved under her door, she grimaced. Who was the hateful man and why had he beaten her?

She rubbed her hand gingerly over her forehead, feeling the lump, and shivered. Her whole body ached. Ever so slowly, she crawled from bed and shuffled to the window. Peering down, she was overcome with relief when she saw Simon and Andrew in the chicken coop gathering eggs.

Glancing toward the barn, her heart lurched. She grabbed the windowsill to steady her weak knees and stared at Noah Schlabach, carrying feed toward the barn. Evidently, her dream had been real.

Moving as quickly as her groaning body would allow, she washed her face and hands and slipped into her dress. After sweeping her tangled hair into a bun, she covered it with her *kapp*, wiped her muddied feet clean and donned her shoes. She hurried into the hallway and inhaled the aroma of fresh-brewed coffee. Surely her imagination was playing tricks on her. The coffee tin had been empty for two weeks.

She gripped the banister and descended the stairs, her aching muscles and strained back objecting to every step. The smell of fried bacon assailed her. Bacon was a luxury she had not tasted in months.

Entering the kitchen, she stopped short as the back door opened and Noah stepped inside. Tall, muscular, more mature and even more handsome.

She swallowed down the lump that filled her throat and stared at the man she had once loved. "I—I…" she stammered. "I thought seeing you last night had been a dream."

"How's your head?" he asked, his voice warm with concern.

Her head was throbbing with frustration, but she refused to let him know how much seeing him unsettled her. "I have a headache. Otherwise, I'm fine."

In spite of her tight muscles, she straightened her spine and narrowed her gaze. "Did I not ask you last night why you came back?"

His mouth twitched, revealing dimples that used to play with her heart. "You did ask me that question."

"I remember dreaming I saw you, then I woke to find you hauling feed to my barn." She rubbed her forehead. "My mind is a bit fuzzy this morning, and I cannot recall your answer. Why did you return to Amish Mountain?"

"Someone wants to buy my father's property. I'm here to sign the papers. Although after what happened last night, I'm not sure why anyone would want to live on the mountain."

"Some of us do not have the luxury of moving," she said with a huff.

"Sorry. As you probably remember, I was never known for my diplomacy." He stepped toward the stove, poured two cups of coffee and handed one to her. "Who beat you up, Ruthie?"

"It was not a social visit," she said, still irritated by his earlier comment. "We did not exchange names."

"The fire was started with gasoline. If not for the rain…" He shrugged. Both of them knew what could have happened.

Had *Gott* intervened? If so, maybe He cared about her and her boys, after all.

Ruthie raised the cup with shaky hands, then sipped the coffee, appreciating the rich brew she had missed, and stared at her near-empty pantry. "Where did you find coffee beans?"

"At my dad's place."

"Along with bacon?" She glanced at the cast-iron skillet warming on the back of the stove.

He lifted his eyebrows, a ploy Simon used when he wanted to make a point. "You used to like bacon."

"That was ten years ago, Noah. A lot has changed since then."

"I remember you were the prettiest girl in the entire area."

She sealed her ears to his sweet talk. She had been fooled once but would not be fooled again.

"I wanted you to go with me that night, Ruthie."

"You were young, Noah, and tired of being Amish." She grimaced inwardly. Because of Noah, she had almost walked away from her faith. How different life would have been if she had left with him.

The sounds of the boys' voices filtered into the kitchen.

"You've raised two fine sons." The word *sons* hung in the air. "Why didn't you tell me you were pregnant?"

The hurt and rejection she had felt so long ago bubbled up anew. She squared her shoulders defiantly. "I did tell you as soon as I realized what was happening to my body. I wrote you immediately and then wrote again and again. Why did you never answer my letters?"

"What?"

"You heard me, Noah. I did not know your address so I took letters to your father and asked him to mail them to you. I expected a reply, even if you did not want to acknowledge our son."

His eyes widened. "I never got any letters."

"Perhaps you forgot."

"Having a son is not something a man would forget."

She glanced away, unwilling to argue. Noah had made his decision all those years ago. She could not change what had happened then, but she would protect her son now. Simon had lost one father. He did not need to know he had a biological father, as well. Especially one that would stay a few days and then move on with his life. A life without his newfound son.

Needing to hide her upset, she went to the cabinet and pulled out four plates, then set the table and filled glasses with water for the boys.

"I brought milk." He pointed to the icebox. "And packed the box with more ice."

"Did you check my pantry last night as well as my icehouse before you headed home?"

"I spent the night on your porch to ensure the attacker did not return. Once the sun came up, I felt you and the boys would be safe while I made a quick trip home for a few supplies."

Although touched by his thoughtfulness, she needed

to remain strong. "Thank you, Noah, but I did not ask for your help."

"I'm well aware of that, Ruthie. You always were a bit stubborn as well as independent."

His words stung. "Stubborn because I did not run away from my responsibility? My father needed me."

"Didn't your husband come first?"

She bristled. "What do you mean?"

"I read about your wedding in *The Budget* newspaper. Ben Eicher wasn't from around here. Why did you both stay on the mountain instead of returning to his home?"

A good question, and one she should have asked before they married. Although a woman in her fourth month of pregnancy needed a father for her unborn child and could not be particular.

Marrying Ben had been a mistake, she had learned quickly, but by then she had been baptized and had committed fully to living the Amish way. No matter how Ben treated her, Amish women did not leave their husbands. Even husbands caught in addiction.

"Ben knew my father needed help," she said in defense of a husband who did not deserve to be defended. At first she had not known he was a gambler, although it did not take long for her to realize the little money they had disappeared whenever Ben went to town. Still, she did not want Noah to know the truth about her husband and their dysfunctional marriage.

"Your father had a brother," Noah stated.

"Yah." She nodded. "My uncle Henry owns a bit of land south of here, but he left the area years ago."

"Perhaps he didn't think your family farm was worth saving, Ruthie," he continued, no doubt unaware of her upset.

"Is that what you told your father when you and Seth ran away in the middle of the night?"

Noah's face tightened.

The pain of learning he had left without her washed over Ruthie again. She had been naive to think Noah would change his plans for her. All she had wanted was a few days until she mustered the courage to tell her father she was leaving. Why had Noah not understood her need to wait?

"You have not mentioned your brother." Regretting her sharp tongue, Ruthie steered the conversation away from the past. "Did he return to the mountain, too?"

"Seth died, Ruthie. It's been almost six months."

The two brothers had been inseparable. Ruthie's heart broke for Noah. She lowered her gaze. "Forgive me. I did not know."

The kitchen door opened, and the boys bounded inside. "We found eggs." Andrew held up his basket. "Lots of them."

Noah tousled Andrew's hair and smiled at Simon. "Enjoy breakfast, boys." He stepped toward the open door. "I've got a couple of jobs to do outside."

"But you need to eat." Though relieved that Noah was leaving, she also wanted him to stay.

"I'm not hungry." Cool air swirled into the kitchen. "After breakfast, boys, come outside and we'll finish the chores."

"Go home, Noah," Ruthie suggested. "Get some sleep. We can manage without you."

He stared at her for a long moment. "You're managing, Ruthie, that's true. But I'm here for a few days. Let me help."

"Then you will leave again?"

"At least this time, I'll know who I'm leaving behind."

"What did he mean?" Andrew asked after Noah had closed the door behind him.

She ignored her son's question. "Wash your hands, boys, and put the bread on the table. We will have bacon along with our eggs."

Simon neared the window and peered outside. "He went into *Datt*'s workshop."

A warning tugged at Ruthie's heart. "I thought you locked the door."

Simon shrugged. "Maybe I forgot. We never used to lock it."

But things had changed.

Before she could answer, Simon added, "That man last night could have been here before."

She stepped closer. "Why do you say that?"

"I saw a man near the river last week."

A nervous thread tangled along her spine. "You did not tell me."

"He asked where the fish were biting. I told him downstream a bit. Funny, though—he did not have a fishing pole."

"What did he look like?"

Simon shrugged. "He stood in the shadow of a tree and held his hand up so I could not see his face."

"Did he leave right away?" she asked, trying to keep her voice even.

"After he asked who was buried on the hill."

Ruthie's heart thumped a warning. "What did you tell him?"

"I told him about *Datt* and *Dawdy*."

"About the accident?"

He nodded.

She would not fault her son, but Simon had revealed that she and the boys lived alone. Was the man who seemed interested in fishing the same man who had attacked her last night?

The sound of someone chopping wood drew her to the window. Simon and Andrew followed. As the three of them peered outside, Noah raised an ax over his head and then, with a powerful downward movement, split a log in two.

Andrew stood on tiptoe, his eyes wide. "Noah brought Simon and me moon pies this morning before you were awake, *Mamm*."

Moon pies had been Noah's favorite as a kid, although his *datt* rarely allowed such a frivolous waste of money. In spite of being Amish, Reuben Schlabach preferred to spend his hard-earned cash on liquid libations. Her own father called Noah's dad a drunk. Ruthie had considered him an unhappy man who regretted the life he had made for himself.

"Even after eating moon pies, I know you are hungry." She shooed the boys toward the sink. "Wash your hands."

Simon reached for the bar of soap. "Did I meet Noah when I was a child?"

A child? She almost laughed. Nine years old, and Simon was trying to be a man. "Noah left the area ten years ago. I do not recall him returning to the mountain until now."

Both boys lathered their hands with soap and rinsed them with the well water.

Simon reached for the towel. "Noah looks like someone I know, but I cannot remember who."

Ruthie's stomach tightened. The boys enjoyed looking at their reflections in the clothing-store mirror the few times they had gone shopping in town. Simon might not realize the truth yet, but as much as he resembled Noah, he would learn who his real *datt* was before long.

Noah was leaving, but would he leave soon enough?

* * *

As frustrated as he felt, Noah could have chopped down an entire forest. Ruthie needed wood so she could cook and keep her house warm. She needed other things, too. Her pantry was almost bare. He had checked the ice-house and found only a few pounds of frozen meat.

Thankfully, he had purchased hamburger and steaks when he was in town, so he was able to leave her enough beef in the icehouse for a few meals. He would return to town for more supplies as soon as possible.

In spite of the cool morning, he worked up a sweat before putting down the ax when the boys hurried outside. Andrew wore a milk mustache and had to run back inside for his hat.

"My brother wants to split wood, Mr. Noah. *Mamm* says he is too young to use an ax."

"She doesn't want him to get hurt. He'll be old enough soon." Noah's heart warmed as he glanced at his son, slender and gangly with big feet and hands. Given time, Simon might grow taller than Noah.

"Have you split wood before, Simon?"

The boy nodded. "Sometimes I help *Mamm*. The ax gives her blisters that hurt her hands, but she never complains."

Forever stoic, Ruthie had also never complained about her infirmed father or her need to care for him.

Noah handed Simon the ax. "You chop while I stack. We'll work together."

The boy's face brightened. *"Yah, gut."*

"Just remember to spread your feet apart as wide as your shoulders and keep your eyes on the wood you plan to split."

Simon gripped the ax, adjusted his stance and glanced at Noah for approval.

"Move your feet out a bit," he advised.

The boy responded.

He raised the ax and brought it down into the middle of the log, splitting the wood on the first swing.

"Good job."

Simon puffed out his chest with the praise.

Before he could grab a second piece of wood, the kitchen door opened and Ruthie stepped onto the porch.

"Simon," she called.

The boy looked up.

"Stack the wood. Then you and Andrew fill the mare's trough with feed. Make sure she has water."

With a sigh, he handed the ax to Noah.

As the boy started to gather the wood, Noah stepped toward the porch where Ruthie stood. "He did a good job."

"You should have asked me first, Noah."

"I chopped wood when I was Simon's age."

"*Yah*, you did a lot of things, but you are not my son."

Simon was *his* son, too, but he didn't deserve the title of Dad. Not now. Not ever. Not when he had turned his back on the boy. Although, in his own defense, he hadn't even known he had a son.

Ruthie must have seen the confusion in his gaze because she came down the steps and put her hand on his arm. "You do not need to fill a role you have never known."

"A boy needs a father."

"Simon will grow into a strong man even though Ben is gone."

Her words cut him like a knife.

"Come inside," she said. "I kept a plate of food warm."

He shook his head and pointed to a distant pasture. "Some of those fence posts look ready to topple. The boys can help me. You don't want to lose the few head of cattle you have."

"Ben planned to sell them at market, but he died, and I…"

She glanced at the grave site, her face tight with emotion. Noah saw the grief she still carried.

"Simon mentioned your father died, too."

Ruthie nodded.

"I'm sorry."

"*Danki*, Noah."

He turned his gaze back to the pasture. "You could slaughter one of your steers for meat," he suggested, hoping to turn the topic away from the deaths of her father and her husband. "Your ice is low. We might be able to have some delivered from town."

She shook her head. "Not this month."

Was money the issue?

He noted the way she steeled her jaw with determination, trying to hold on to her pride. Ruthie was doing her best to provide for her boys.

He glanced at the peeling paint on the house and outbuildings, and the dilapidated barn. No matter how hard she tried, it wasn't enough.

"I've decided to go to town tomorrow. Why don't you and the boys join me? You could tell the sheriff about your visitor last night and any details you might have remembered."

"Everything happened so quickly." She wrapped her arms around her slender waist.

"Is there something the man might want that is yours? Or could he be an acquaintance of your husband?"

"An *Englisch* lady's stocking covered his head so I could not see his face. Simon told me about a man at the riverbank last week who asked where to fish."

"A sportsman wanting a tip on where to toss his line?"

"Maybe, except he did not have a fishing pole, and he wanted to know who was buried on the hill."

Noah turned toward the graves. "Your husband is buried there?"

She nodded. "Along with my mother and father."

"You and the boys shouldn't be left alone, Ruthie. I'll bed down in the barn tonight."

"As ramshackle as it is, the barn might collapse on top of you."

He smiled. "Then I'll sleep on your porch again."

"You have already done enough, Noah. Besides, I would worry about you if you stayed outside in the cold. Go home and rest. With the doors locked, the boys and I will be safe in the house."

"I heard the dinner bell last night. Ring it if you need me."

"Do not worry about us. We will be fine."

But he was worried. A man had attacked Ruthie once. Noah had to ensure he did not hurt her a second time.

THREE

Noah kept thinking about Ruthie and her two sons when he returned home later that evening. After eating dinner, he brewed coffee and took a cup onto the porch, listening to the hoot of a night owl and the scamper of squirrels burrowing through the underbrush.

He also heard the flow of the river. Rain had fallen intermittently all afternoon and more was expected over the next few days. He and the boys had shored up the pasture fence in between the hardest downpours. Other repairs needed to be tackled in the morning.

Ruthie might think she could handle the farm, but it was too much for her. The boys were good workers and helped as best they could, but they couldn't fill the gap left by Ben Eicher's passing. Although from the level of disrepair Noah had noticed, Ruthie's husband had failed to keep up the farm. Years of neglect under her father's hand had been, no doubt, compounded by a lackadaisical husband.

Noah finished the coffee and returned the mug to the kitchen, then grabbed his keys, climbed into his truck and headed toward the bridge. Thankfully, the water level had lowered a bit with the ease in the rainfall. He checked the bridge's underpinnings, and decided to brace the support beams as best he could tomorrow.

Leaving his truck on the far bank, he walked across the bridge to get a better view of the Plank farm, now shadowed in darkness. An oil lamp glowed in a downstairs window of the farmhouse, inviting him forward. He hurried to the porch and tapped on the door.

"Ruthie, it's Noah."

She opened the door. "Is everything all right?"

Her hair hung loose around her shoulders. A small triangular scarf covered her head and was tied under her chin, in lieu of her prayer *kapp*.

"I decided to check your property but didn't want to scare you. Are the boys asleep?"

She nodded. "They were exhausted after working with you today."

"I appreciated their help."

"And the questions?" Her eyes almost twinkled in the lamplight. "The boys are much too inquisitive."

His heart warmed as he thought of their nonstop chatter this afternoon. "Curious minds are quick to learn. They both take after their mother in that regard."

She raised an eyebrow and smiled. "Are you saying I was talkative in my youth?"

He laughed. "I'm referring to intelligence, Ruthie. You're a smart woman."

"A smart woman should be able to manage this farm better than I am currently doing."

"Your husband and father haven't been gone long." He looked expectantly at her.

"Two months." She let out a shallow sigh. "In some ways it seems like only yesterday, yet when I look around the farm, I feel it has been neglected for years."

"Any sign of the guy from last night?" he asked.

"Everything has been quiet."

"Good." He glanced over his shoulder at the rocky terrain. "I'll search around the outbuildings and ensure nothing is amiss in the barn."

She motioned toward the living area. "If you would like to come inside for a cup of coffee afterward—"

He held up his hand. "I'll take a rain check."

"Then good night, and thank you."

Standing on the porch as she closed the door, Noah felt a weight settle on his shoulders. Everything within him begged to accept her offer. He wanted to learn who Ruthie Eicher was. He had known Ruthie Plank, but ten years was a long time. He had changed. No doubt, she had, as well.

With a deep sigh, he left the porch and searched the barn. The wood shop and other outbuildings were locked. He glanced over the pastures and the hillside, then walked back across the bridge and climbed into his pickup. For a long moment, he stared at Ruthie's house.

His father, in one of his drunken stupors, had mocked Noah, calling him a protector who wanted to keep everyone safe. The irony cut Noah to the quick after what had happened to Seth, his wife, Jeanine, and their adorable daughter, Mary.

Seth had never been happier than when he and Noah had worked on the dam near Chattanooga. After carefully saving enough money, Seth and Jeanine had placed a down payment on their starter home and had invited Noah to dinner that first night in the new house to share in their joy. The pride Noah had felt in his little brother had made his heart nearly burst.

Two weeks later, the dam gave way, and a wall of water washed over the housing area as the family slept.

Noah had worked on the dam. He had gotten Seth a job there and had told him about the new houses being built and the low-interest loans for people employed by the construction company.

If Noah hadn't been so helpful, Seth and his family would still be alive.

He started the engine and turned the truck around. Noah had come home to sell his father's property. The real-estate agent had a buyer. Tomorrow in town, he would see if the papers had been drawn up. Noah needed to move on with his life. There was nothing except memories on Amish Mountain.

Then he thought of Ruthie and Simon and little Andrew. His heart softened, yet he needed to be realistic. Although he had left the Amish faith before baptism, Noah had lived life as an *Englischer* for the past ten years. Amish and *Englisch* didn't mix, at least not when romantic relationships were concerned. There could be no going back to what they'd had so long ago.

Plus, he didn't deserve happiness or love or a family, and had to make certain he didn't get involved. Bottom line—the sooner he left the mountain, the better.

Ruthie extinguished the oil lamp and moved to the window. In the moonlight, she watched Noah walk over the bridge, climb into his truck and sit there for a long moment. Was he thinking of her or their son?

She had said too much about their circumstances. She did not want Noah to know they were hanging on by a thread. A very thin thread. Surely he would wonder about the Amish community and why they were not reaching out to the widow Eicher.

Truth be told, she had rejected their help. The shame of Ben's gambling and subsequent shunning pained her to the core, even after all this time, and the memory of his outrage during Sunday service haunted her still. Ben had called the bishop and elders hypocrites and stormed out. Ruthie had gathered the boys and followed him, holding her head high. All the while, her face had burned with shame.

Her father had always said a wife's place was beside

her husband. If Ben was shunned, then she felt shunned, as well. Even after his death, she had not been able to embrace the community or accept their outreach.

After his shunning, Ben had gone to town once a month to gamble, collect the mail at the post office and buy supplies with whatever money was left after his poker games. She and the boys had remained at home to handle the chores. All too often, she had prayed her husband would not return. *Gott* forgive her for such thoughts.

Ben always returned in a foul mood, as if he had been forced home to a wife he did not love and an elder son he knew was not his own. At times, she wondered why he had married her. Was it for her father's farm or had he believed love could grow between them? After Simon's birth, Ben claimed the baby was the problem, but she knew the problem was Ben, who usually thought only of himself.

Ruthie turned from the window, carried her cup to the sink, washed it and placed it in the cupboard, her thoughts moving back to Noah and the way he had brought joy to her life when they were young. They had played together as children, and with time that friendship had grown into something more. Ruthie had been too free with her love, which she regretted, yet she never regretted the wonderful child who had come from their youthful tryst.

Footsteps sounded on the porch. Her heart fluttered. Noah had come back to see her.

Not waiting for his knock, she threw open the door.

"Oh, Noah, I am glad—"

Her heart lurched. The man with the stocking over his head was not Noah. Before she could slam the door, he pushed his way into the house. She gasped.

"What are you waiting for?" He leaned into her face. "Time is running out."

She squared her shoulders and steadied her voice. "What are you talking about?"

"Move off the mountain. No one wants you here."

"That is not true."

His eyes widened. "Are you calling me a liar?"

"I am calling you a fool to think you can frighten me."

"I'll make life miserable for you and your children."

He raised his hand as if to strike her. She grabbed his arm, and his shirtsleeve raised, revealing tattoos that covered his skin.

His face contorted, and he pushed her away with such force that she tumbled to the floor, landing on her hip. Pain ricocheted up her spine.

She struggled to her feet, knowing she had to be strong to protect her boys.

"Get out of here." She pointed to the door. "Leave me alone."

"I told you what will happen if you don't get off Amish Mountain."

Seething with anger, he stepped closer. "Don't make a tragic mistake if you want your boys to live."

He shoved her hard against a table and ran outside.

Ruthie stumbled and fell to her knees, overcome with a mix of confusion and fear.

Once again, footsteps sounded on the porch.

Her heart pounded. He was coming back.

She grabbed the edge of the table and tried to stand. She had to keep him from harming Simon and Andrew.

His footfalls drew closer.

She screamed.

Arms surrounded her. "Ruthie!"

Gasping, she collapsed into Noah's arms.

"He—he came back. He said he would…kill my boys. Help me, Noah. Help me save my boys."

FOUR

Noah held Ruthie close until she calmed. Having her in his arms tugged on his heart. So many memories flooded over him and reminded him how dearly he had loved Ruthie once upon a time. Now someone was doing her harm.

"Why is this man coming after you?" he asked once she moved out of his embrace.

She shook her head and cast her eyes down. "It is difficult to discuss."

"You mentioned coffee earlier," he suggested, hoping to ease her tension. "A cup would be good for both of us."

"*Yah*, you are right. I brewed a pot early and kept it on the stove so it will still be hot." She led the way into the kitchen and poured the coffee. After opening a cabinet drawer, she lifted out a large manila envelope, carried it to the table along with the filled cups and sat across from Noah.

"I do not want you to think badly about my husband, but it is necessary to tell you some things so you understand what is happening." She stared at the envelope and then glanced up at Noah.

"Perhaps you have already heard talk in town?" she asked.

"I didn't talk to anyone about you, Ruthie. I thought your father was still alive and that you and your husband lived elsewhere."

"If you had asked, you would have heard that my husband liked to gamble."

Noah saw the pain on her face.

"What started as an occasional problem grew worse with time," she admitted.

Noah took her hand. "I'm sorry."

"The hardest part was his disregard for the boys, especially Simon. Not that Ben was a better father to Andrew."

"He knew you were pregnant when you married?"

She nodded and pulled back her hand. "I was truthful. He said it did not matter that I was in the family way, but it did matter. Evidently more than either of us realized."

Her words cut into Noah. The thought of Simon being raised by a man who didn't love him was almost too much to bear. Noah carried the guilt for the deaths of his brother's family. To learn that he was also responsible for a child who had been slighted by his stepfather weighed him down even more.

"What about the church district?" he asked. "Did the bishop not offer counsel?"

"Ben did not accept criticism or advice, even from the bishop. When Andrew was a baby, my husband caused a disruption during Sunday services while the bishop was speaking. Ben called him a hypocrite and said all the elders were ungodly men who preached lies."

"Oh, Ruthie, how that must have hurt you."

She wrung her hands. "Ben said he wanted nothing more to do with the church. Because of his gambling and his disregard for the bishop's counsel, he was removed from the faith, just as he wanted."

"You mean *Bann* and *Meidung*?"

"*Yah*. He was excommunicated and shunned."

"But you weren't. Surely the bishop would not hold what your husband did against you."

"I was Ben's wife. If he was cut off from the community, I was, too."

"You could have asked for help."

She glanced at him, her eyes revealing the shame she must have felt for all these years.

"As you know, Noah, we live on the mountain, far from town. What do the *Englisch* say? Out of sight, out of mind."

He nodded. The townspeople had not made an effort to help Ruthie because of her husband.

"Although to be honest, a few people checked on me after the incident in church. Following Ben's death, they reached out to me again, but I was still too shamed by my husband's actions as well as his shunning and refused their help."

"How does all this have bearing on what's happening now?" he asked.

She glanced again at the envelope. "Ben would go to town once a month to get the mail and to gamble."

Her voice was little more than a whisper. "The last time he went to town, my father went with him. My *datt*'s health was bad. He had grown so frail. I asked Ben to take him to the medical clinic for an exam, which I am certain interfered with Ben's gambling. On the way home, he raced through an intersection and never saw the approaching car that had the right of way."

"They both died in the collision."

Ruthie nodded. "Comforting the boys was hard. They did not understand how *Gott* could take both their father and their grandfather. Some people said it was *Gott*'s will, but that is difficult for children to comprehend."

She paused for a moment and then added, "It was difficult for me to accept, as well."

"You've been through so much, Ruthie."

"It is life, *yah*? We are given both the good and the bad. How we act in those difficult situations can either build strength or tear us down. I am determined to remain strong."

"You have always been strong and faithful to the Lord. You're showing the boys how a *gut* person lives, and they learn well from your example."

"I fear they are now learning how a hateful man can ruin a family's peace and well-being." She withdrew a piece of paper from the envelope, unfolded it and placed it on the table.

Pointing to the paper, she said, "This is what I found under my door two weeks ago. It states that I need to leave the farm."

Noah read what appeared to be a hastily scribbled note written in green ink. "Do you recognize the handwriting or the color of the ink?"

She shook her head. "Several days ago another note was slipped under my door."

Withdrawing the second slip of paper from the envelope, she sighed. "This one is also written in green ink and says I would be sorry if I did not leave within forty-eight hours."

Noah looked at the date on the second letter. "And the fire occurred last night as the deadline lapsed?"

She nodded. "I did not realize he would be so hateful. I fear evil has taken over his heart."

Noah tried to think why this property would be so important.

Ruthie folded the papers and returned them to the envelope. "The man talks about hurting my children. That is what frightens me."

"We need to tell the sheriff."

"And what will he do? Willkommen is far from the mountain. My children and I live here alone. I have no phone to call for help."

"Cell reception is almost impossible on the mountain,

Ruthie. I've had trouble trying to make calls since I returned home, but if you need to contact anyone, you can try my phone."

"I cannot rely on you, Noah. You are here now, but you will leave as soon as your father's land is sold. I do not blame you. As you said, why would anyone want to live on Amish Mountain? It is true, but it is the only thing I have to call my own, other than my wonderful sons. I want to pass this farm on to them. Without the land, how would I grow food or raise chickens and have eggs? There is so much work to do with a farm, but I want to raise my children on this mountain."

As much as Noah admired Ruthie's determination, he knew she would be an easy target for the man who had come after her. Noah needed to talk her out of staying, but since he hadn't been able to convince Ruthie to leave years ago, he doubted he could convince her to leave now.

Perhaps there had been more to her staying back then than just caring for her father. The Amish felt a kinship with the land. It provided their livelihood, their food, their ability to sustain life.

In his youth, Noah hadn't been aware of Ruthie's love of the land. Now that he had nothing of his own and no one to hold on to, he could understand her desire to remain on the farm that had belonged to her family for generations.

He thought of his own guilt in his brother's tragic death. Noah had no right to find comfort in his childhood home and surrounding property. He would sell it all and continue to wander from job to job, even if a portion of his heart remained on the mountain, as it had so long ago.

Ruthie could not sleep. Every time she closed her eyes, she envisioned the man with the distorted face and the tattooed arm. Discouraged and upset, she rose from bed and walked to the window. A light from Noah's house glowed in the darkness. Perhaps he, too, was trying to make sense of her tangled life.

She had not wanted to tell Noah about her husband. The mistake of marrying Ben had been her own to make. She did not need pity, or for Noah to feel responsible for the struggles she had endured. Life had to be accepted, no matter how difficult. Ben often told her if she was a better wife, he would have been a better husband. Not that she understood his logic. Whenever he spoke such nonsense, she would busy herself with cooking or cleaning and steel her heart to his criticism. Her father had never offered praise and his words had been caustic at times, but Ben's belligerence was different, and no matter how hard she tried to shrug off his comments, they troubled her spirit and sapped the joy from her life.

What hurt her even more is that she had tried to be a dutiful wife, but Ben's verbal attacks on her worth as a person, as well as a wife, took a toll until her heart had hardened.

If she had her boys, she had everything she needed. Keeping the farm was for their future, so she could provide something other than the memory of their childhood with a father who did not know how to love.

She stared again at the light in the distance. Once upon a time, she had been in love. She loved her children, but she would never be able to love a man again. No matter how much she remembered the past and what Noah had meant to her then.

Ten years was a lifetime. She had changed, not necessarily for the better. She accepted her life as it was and did not need to run from the pain. Joy had been part of her distant past, before Noah left the mountain, but it would not be part of her future.

FIVE

Noah had breakfast ready by the time Ruthie came downstairs the next morning. He poured a cup of coffee and handed it to her when she stepped into the kitchen.

"Looks like you could use a little caffeine."

"I need more than caffeine." She accepted the cup with a weak smile and took a long sip.

"You'll find the spare key on the counter," he said. "Thanks for letting me keep it overnight."

"I gave it to you in case there was an emergency. I did not expect you to cook breakfast for us."

"It's the least I could do. Plus, I'm worried about you. It might be wise to have a doc check you over, Ruthie. I told you that I plan to go to town today to get some supplies to work on your barn. Come with me."

"No. I am stiff and sore, but nothing is broken and I will be good as new in a few days."

He could see the dark lines under her eyes and the way she held her side. Ruthie was tough. Always had been.

"And you do not need to fix my barn," she insisted.

"I've got the time and the wherewithal. Plus it gives me a chance to spend time with Simon and Andrew."

"I am sure you have other things to do."

"Not until my father's house is sold. I'll check with the real-estate agent today. I called his office when I first arrived in town. His receptionist said it would take a week to get everything ready. I might hurry them along if I stop in today."

"You would not want to stay on the mountain longer than necessary."

He heard the subtle hint of sarcasm in her voice and raised his brow.

She ignored his gaze and took another sip of coffee, then placed the cup on the table. "The boys will be downstairs soon. Thank you for preparing breakfast."

"Breakfast is easy. I'm sorry I couldn't stop the man from hurting you last night."

The boys scurried downstairs and bounded into the kitchen. Andrew's eyes widened. "What smells so *gut*?"

"Noah has fixed us breakfast." Ruthie's smile was warm. "Come sit at the table, and I will pour your milk."

"But the chores," Simon insisted.

"I've cared for the animals," Noah assured him. "We can work together on the other jobs after we eat. It won't take us long." He pointed to the table. "Sit next to your brother. We'll eat while the food is warm."

Simon slipped into his chair. "My stomach is ready to eat."

"Mine, too," Andrew said, holding out his glass for his mother to fill.

"Noah has brought us many good things to eat, as well as milk to drink. What do you boys say?"

"*Danki*, Noah," they chimed in unison.

"It is *gut* to enjoy a meal with my neighbors." He placed a large platter of sausages and scrambled eggs in the center of the table. A smaller plate was piled high with buttered toast.

"Bacon yesterday and sausage today. It is like Christmas." Andrew took a long chug from his glass, then wiped his mouth with the back of his hand.

"Use your napkin," Ruthie instructed. "And we will wait for Noah to join us before we give thanks."

Noah hadn't asked the Lord to bless his food since his mother had died. His father had rarely sat at the table to eat following her passing, and Noah and Seth had quickly forsaken many of the Amish ways, including prayer before meals.

Simon and Andrew waited expectantly for him to sit. Sliding into the seat opposite Ruthie, he smiled at the boys. "Shall we bow our heads in prayer?"

They dutifully followed his suggestion, their eyes closed and faces serene. His heart warmed at their innocence. He turned his gaze to Ruthie. She stared at him, one eyebrow arched ever so slightly, as if questioning what he was doing coming back into her life.

Noah glanced down, mentally trying to calm his rapid heartbeat. Unable to focus on prayer, he pulled in a breath and quieted his mind. He needed to ensure his heart didn't get carried away with thoughts of Ruthie.

Bless her, he silently intoned. *And her children.*

He raised his eyes to find the boys staring at him and winked at Simon. "Shall we eat?"

Handing the large platter to Ruthie, he said, "Serve the boys and yourself first."

She arranged the food on the three plates and then offered it once again to Noah. "Breakfast looks delicious."

"At times it's nice to have someone else do the cooking." He glanced at the boys. "Simon and Andrew, you need to learn to cook so you can fix breakfast for your *mamm.*"

"We do the outside chores," Andrew said, reaching for his fork.

"And you're good workers. I could tell that yesterday."

Simon spread jam on a slice of toast. "Your eye, *Mamm*. It looks worse today."

She glanced at Noah. "A bruise comes a day or two after the injury. Do not worry about your *mamm*."

"I do not want to see you hurt."

She patted his hand. "You are a *gut* son."

Noah's stomach tightened. A *gut* son who needed a man's guidance. Andrew needed that, as well.

Ruthie didn't want the boys to know the stranger had returned last night. Noah had to make certain the man didn't have another opportunity to hurt her again. What type of an animal would attack a defenseless woman? His stomach soured as he thought of what could have happened.

The boys were enjoying the food with enthusiasm. Again he thought of the pain the attack could have caused to both Simon and Andrew.

Much as he wanted to go to town today, he wouldn't leave Ruthie and the boys alone. Not when the vile man was on the loose. If only Ruthie and the boys would go to town with him.

"Noah plans to go to town today," Ruthie said as if reading his thoughts. "Would you boys like to join him?"

"Oh, *yah*," both boys enthused.

"It has been so long since we have gone anywhere," Simon said, serious as always and sounding much older than his years.

"Today will be an adventure, *yah*?" Ruthie smiled.

"What about the chores?" Simon asked.

"We'll do them before we leave," Noah assured him.

Ruthie nodded. "Finish your food and the three of you can head outside, while I tidy the kitchen. Many hands make light work."

"This day could not be better." Andrew downed the rest

of his milk and finished the last of the eggs on his plate. "A *gut* breakfast and a trip to town make me very happy."

"What if the man returns while we are gone?" Simon asked, his brow wrinkled with worry.

"We will lock the doors to the house and will not think about him anymore today."

"I think of him when I see the bruise on your face."

"Then I must heal quickly so looking at your *mamm* does not upset you."

"That is not what I mean."

She nodded. "I understand, Simon. None of us want to see the man again, but we cannot live life in fear. We have to trust *Gott* to keep us safe."

"He did not keep you safe night before last."

"No, but the fire in the woodpile did not spread and nothing of significance burned. *Gott* protected us in that way, even if he allowed the man to hurt me."

"Bad things sometimes happen," Noah said, hoping to deflect the boy's upset. "But as your mother said, it could have been so much worse."

Simon squared his shoulders. "I will not let him hurt her again."

Noah admired Simon's determination and desire to protect his mother. For all his good intentions, Simon wouldn't be a match for an adult who weighed more and was, no doubt, adept at bullying people, especially defenseless women and children.

"You'll let me know, Simon, if you see anything suspicious, *yah*? We'll work together as a team to keep your mother safe."

"Can I be on your team?" Andrew asked.

"Of course. We three men will protect your mother." He nodded to Ruthie. "Now let's take the dishes to the sink, then we'll get our chores done and be ready for our trip to town."

"Are we taking the buggy?" Simon asked.

"I am sure our mare, Buttercup, would enjoy the trip," Ruthie said. "We will go by buggy."

The boys cleared the table and then hurried outside.

"I hate leaving you to wash the dishes," Noah said.

"They will not take long. Do you want me to pack a lunch?"

"If the boys like pizza, we can eat in town."

"You are spoiling them, Noah. What will I do with them when you are gone?"

Although her tone was light, her gaze was serious.

"We won't think about that now. Today is for enjoyment, *yah*?"

"Of course, Noah. Today will be a nice change, but we will remember that your time here will be short-lived. Soon you will leave, and we will go back to life as it was."

Noah's life would never be the same. From now on when he thought of Ruthie, he would also think of the son he only recently learned he had and the boy's brother. Both Amish lads needed an Amish father, not an *Englischer* who had left the faith.

Ruthie tried to calm her excitement. Going to town had been a rarity when Ben was alive. Since his death, she had too much work to do on the farm to think about leaving for even a few hours.

The boys shared her enthusiasm. Both of them scrambled into the buggy, talking about what they would see and do in Willkommen.

Noah seemed as pleased as the boys, and said, "It will be a fun day," as he flicked the reins and guided the mare onto the mountain road.

The weather was perfect. Sunny and bright, which matched Ruthie's mood. She had worn her black bonnet and pulled it around her face in hopes of hiding the bruise around her eye. Her ribs ached but not bad enough to be broken, and that was something else for which to be grateful.

"I checked the barn again this morning to determine what's needed to shore it up," Noah told her.

"Did you see the wood piled behind Ben's woodshop?"

He nodded. "I did. From the looks of the lumber, your husband was preparing to do the job himself. I'll just need a few more items before I start work."

"We can help you," Simon said from the rear.

"I'm counting on that."

Ruthie was grateful for the way Noah included her sons in the project. Ben had preferred tackling a job alone rather than guiding young hands through a new task. He had always been less than patient with their sons and with her.

"Age has given you the gift of patience," she said to Noah. Then she thought of his impatience in leaving Amish Mountain so many years ago. If only he had waited for her.

She turned to glance at the lush mountain scenery, not wanting him to see the confusion that she knew was written on her face. Confusion and pain, even after all these years, because he had left without her.

"I was impetuous in my youth, Ruthie, and for that I'm sorry."

Did he even realize how deeply he had hurt her? She could not think of it again lest the pain overtake her.

"Virtue does not come easily," she mused, hoping to deflect her focus onto something else. "My mother said it takes a lifetime. Unfortunately, she did not have long enough."

"You were always a loving daughter."

The boys chatted in the rear. Ruthie was thankful they had not heard what she and Noah had said. She never should have opened up the wound from her past. Noah would be leaving soon. She did not want to be left with a broken heart again.

Bracing her shoulders, she steeled her resolve. Noah was *Englisch*, she reminded herself, as if that wedge between them was not evident. He had rejected his faith at the same time he had rejected her. There could be no going back to what had been so long ago.

SIX

Noah recognized Ruthie's upset in the way she braced her shoulders and held her neck at an angle. She turned away from him, just as she'd done the night he wanted her to leave with him. She had used her father as an excuse, and the pain of rejection he felt had been so intense and immediate that Noah had fled the mountain, leaving behind that which he loved most.

In hindsight, his pride and concern for his own well-being had taken precedence over Ruthie's need to care for her father. He had lived with that regret for the last ten years.

With the boys sitting in the buggy, Noah knew this wasn't the time to go into their past. Although he doubted there would ever be a good time. Ruthie had found a husband, a man she loved in spite of his many flaws, and he'd been taken from her and the boys. Noah would be a hypocrite to wade into the midst of her mourning and pretend he could offer her something more. After losing his brother and his brother's sweet wife and adorable daughter, Noah didn't deserve a second chance when Seth had no chance at all.

He flicked the reins, feeling the frustration at his own failings well up in him again. Life wasn't fair. His father used to say that often in the context that others had more land or money or happiness. His dad had tried to find all that he was looking for in a bottle. Noah had chosen to make his own happiness through hard work, but neither of them had succeeded.

"How long until we get to town?" Andrew asked from the rear.

Ruthie turned and smiled. "Are you impatient, my son?"

"*Yah, Mamm.* I have wanted to go to town for so long. Now that it is happening, I am too excited to sit still."

"You must copy Simon and the way he remains quiet."

"Simon is quiet because he is older."

Simon shoved his young brother playfully. "Years do not make the difference. I was born quiet and you were born to talk and wiggle. *Datt* said we were born different."

"Because you are tall and I am short?"

"You will grow, Andrew. *Mamm* said I am ready to grow out of my clothes."

"And your hat and shoes," the younger boy added. "You said they are both too small."

Noah turned to Ruthie. "Perhaps we should stop at the shoe store."

"Spring is almost upon us, and summer will follow soon thereafter. The boys go barefoot when the weather is warm."

Ruthie's pride was keeping her from buying shoes. Pride and a lack of resources.

He lowered his voice to keep the children from hearing. "I would like to buy shoes for Simon. Andrew, too."

She shook her head.

"Think about it."

Upon entering town, he pointed to the real-estate office. "I need to check on the papers for the sale of my property. Do you want to go into the dry-goods store next door?"

Again, he lowered his voice. "Get new straw hats for the boys. If they sell shoes, buy them, too."

"The shoes can wait, Noah, and their old hats are fine."

"*Mamm*, my hat hardly fits," Simon moaned. Evidently he had heard a portion of their conversation.

"Please, Ruthie." Noah leaned closer so the boys could not see the wad of bills he placed into her hand. "Let me do this."

She stared at him for a long moment and then glanced back at Simon. "Noah is right. You both are outgrowing not only your shoes, but also your hats. We will get hats today and shoes at the end of the summer."

"Then it's decided." Noah smiled. "I won't be long. If you need something new, Ruthie, I would be glad to buy all the purchases. You and your family were always there for me when times were tough."

And when his father was on one of his binges, but Noah wouldn't mention that in front of the boys.

"Thank you, Noah. I will pay you back for the hats."

"No need." Except for her pride.

He turned the buggy toward the rear of the store and tied the mare to the hitching post. The boys eagerly jumped down while he helped Ruthie out of the buggy.

"I am not used to such attention," she whispered once her feet touched the pavement.

She stood still for a long moment. He didn't want to move lest the moment passed and she stepped away.

"You deserve attention, Ruthie," he whispered.

"We are no longer young teens, Noah." She turned to gather her sons. "We will see you when you are finished with your real-estate business."

Noah glanced along the street to ensure no one suspect was hovering nearby. The man who had come after

Ruthie at her house was a coward and would hide until darkness, or when she was alone, before he struck again.

Noah would make sure she and the boys weren't left unprotected while he stayed in the area. But as he walked into the real-estate office, he knew he couldn't protect them for long. As soon as the sale of his father's property was final, Noah would leave Amish Mountain.

"Is it Ruthie Eicher I see?" the female clerk asked when Ruthie stepped into the shop with the boys following close behind.

Ruthie's first inclination was to turn around and leave the store, but the boys were excited about their shopping adventure, and she would not let her own desire to stay away from people ruin the day for her sons.

She nodded and stepped closer, trying to identify the Amish woman, near her own age, who had greeted them.

"You do not recognize me?" the clerk asked. "I am Fannie Martin. We went to school together."

The name surprised her since the slender woman standing in front of her looked nothing like the plump Fannie she remembered from her youth. "You are Daniel's sister."

"Yah." The clerk nodded. "I was a year younger and always thought you were the prettiest girl in the school."

Ruthie's cheeks warmed. "You should not say such things, Fannie."

"Of course I should not say them, but still I do. Are these fine boys your sons?"

She nodded, her heart swelling with maternal pride that could not be helped. If pride could ever be positive, it would be a mother's love for her children.

"What can I help you find?" the clerk asked.

"The boys wanted to look at straw hats."

"A shipment came in last week. You will find them on the last aisle in the rear of the store."

The bell over the door rang as another customer stepped inside. Ruthie recognized Sarah Deitweiler, a middle-aged woman with a pinched nose and unsmiling eyes. Sarah had spread rumors around town about Ben's vice. Ruthie sighed at the memory of Sarah's less-than-loving comments. Ruthie's Aunt Mattie, her mother's sister, had tried to ease Ruthie's upset, yet even her aunt found Sarah to be a troublesome gossip.

Not wanting to give Mrs. Deitweiler more fuel for her wagging tongue, Ruthie steered the boys to the back of the shop.

Fannie greeted the newly arrived customer with much fanfare, as if to ensure Sarah Deitweiler's shopping experience would be positive. Word of mouth was the best way to market, the Amish knew, but one disgruntled customer could sour a business's reputation.

"Is that Ruthie Eicher?" the older woman said loud enough to be heard throughout the store.

"You know her?" the cheerful clerk asked.

"I don't associate with her type. In fact, I find it strange that she would show her face in town after everything that happened with her husband."

"Mrs. Deitweiler, a wife is not responsible for her husband's actions," the clerk said in Ruthie's defense.

"You may think that, child, but as you age, you will learn the truth." The older woman harrumphed. "I will leave now to do my grocery shopping and come back to purchase my dry goods another day."

Ruthie glanced down at her sons. Simon's face fell and Andrew's brow furrowed. The boys had overheard the woman's comment just as Ruthie had. She hated seeing their embarrassment.

Did they realize what it meant to be shunned? She had never mentioned their father's tirade, when he had walked out of the Sunday service after calling the bishop and elders hypocrites. Simon had been old enough to re-member the stares of those gathered to worship that day. Now he placed his hand in hers and squeezed as if offer-ing support.

"What people say about us is not important, boys. What is important is what is in our hearts and that we live our lives as *Gott* would want. You do not need to hang your heads or be ashamed. You are fine boys, and I am proud of both of you."

"But the woman did not want to shop when you were in the store," Simon said, pointing out what they both knew to be true.

"We will not try to guess her reason for leaving. In-stead, we will look at hats, which is the purpose for our visit."

Although Ruthie tried to make light of what had hap-pened, the boys had been deflated and their exuberance faltered.

Simon picked out a hat, then peered at the price tag. "My old hat is *gut*, *Mamm*. It keeps the sun from my eyes. I do not need a newer hat that will do the same thing."

"But—" Andrew started to object as he reached for a hat in his size.

Simon took his hand. "Andrew, this is not what we need now. Come, we will go outside and wait for Noah while *Mamm* shops for herself."

Touched by Simon's maturity, and also saddened that he realized how far she had to stretch each dollar, she ush-ered them both toward the door. "I need nothing today," she told the boys. "We will all wait for Noah outside."

The clerk was busy unloading new merchandise and did not see them leave.

Once outside, they sat on a bench near the sidewalk and watched the cars and buggies pass. The sun had gone behind the clouds and the breeze was crisp. Their adventure was off to a less-than-encouraging start.

Seeing Noah exit the real-estate office and hurry toward them, she feared he would have news of the imminent sale of his property. If he announced he was leaving in the next day or two, she would return to the buggy and ask him to take them home.

Instead, Noah smiled as he neared. "Did you find hats?"

"We will wait for another day," Simon answered for both boys.

Noah glanced at her, as if questioning what happened.

"We were not in the mood to shop." She returned his money when the boys were not looking and hoped he would not press for more details.

She had thought the shame of the past would end with Ben's death, but shame lived on even now. She could bear being rejected, but she did not want that for her children.

SEVEN

Noah could sense Ruthie's tension, and he read pain in her eyes. Something had happened in the store that was more upsetting than the price of hats. He wondered if it had to do with small-town gossip.

The boys hung their heads as if finding great interest in the pavement. Simon's shoulders slumped and his mouth drooped. Andrew rested his elbow on the arm of the bench and held his head in his hand. The sadness that covered both boys' faces tugged at Noah's heart. He wanted to wrap them in his embrace and right whatever wrong had happened.

This morning, they had all been so excited about the trip to town. Noah thought the day would be fun and an opportunity to be together. Evidently he had been wrong.

Last night, Ruthie had shared about Ben's past. From his own youth, Noah knew how scathing gossip could be. Some people thrived on spreading hateful tales that harmed not only the people involved, but also innocent bystanders, such as the boys. Neither Andrew nor Simon were responsible for their father's actions, yet they, too, suffered. Life could be unfair. Noah knew that all too well.

"What about your land?" Ruthie asked as if trying to focus on something other than their distasteful experience in the shop.

"The real-estate agent is out of town today. His receptionist said the papers aren't ready. Prescott Construction is the name of the company wishing to buy the property. I thought I'd use the computer in the library to find information on the construction firm."

"The post office is across the street from the library. I would like to get my mail."

"We'll stop there as well as the library."

Simon's eyes widened. "Could you show us how to use a computer?"

"If your mother says it's all right."

Ruthie pursed her lips. "Technology is not something the Amish embrace."

"Please, *Mamm*." Simon grabbed her hand, his earlier upset seemingly forgotten.

Following his older brother's lead, Andrew tugged at her other arm. "The library has books, *Mamm*. You want us to read more."

She nodded. "Books are good. I am not sure about computers."

"You could go to the post office while the boys and I go to the library," Noah suggested. "It won't take long."

"Can you use your phone to search for the information?" she asked.

"I'll have more success using a computer. Plus, Simon and Andrew will enjoy seeing how they work."

Ruthie tilted her head as if mulling over her decision. "You will be careful?"

She was no doubt worried about the man on the mountain. "I'll be as cautious with them as you would be. You can trust me, Ruthie."

She stared at him for a long moment, and he wondered if she was weighing that very point. He had destroyed her trust ten years ago, so he understood her hesitation. The boys sat quietly, seemingly holding their breaths as they awaited her response.

Finally, she nodded. "The boys can stay with you while I get the mail."

Noah almost sighed with relief, but he didn't want the boys to realize what a huge concession their *mamm* had made. Ruthie had guarded her children for so long. He imagined she had placed herself between them and her husband, always the protective mother never wanting anything to hurt her boys.

He had asked Ruthie to trust him. Taking the boys to the library wouldn't seem like anything major to most people, but Noah was grateful that she had placed her sons in his care, even if just for a short time.

"Come on, guys, let's escort your mother to the post office, then we'll head to the library."

The boys skipped ahead as Noah and Ruthie followed behind at a more leisurely pace. Ruthie's shoulders were tense, and she flicked her gaze up and down the street.

She was worried about the man from the mountain. Perhaps she was also worried about whom she would see in town. From what she had told him last night, Ruthie and the boys had remained isolated on the farm and away from townspeople who had witnessed her husband's tirade at that Sunday service prior to his shunning. Undoubtedly, she still carried the scars from her humiliation.

In a way, Noah could relate. As a youth, he and Seth had been ashamed of their father. They heard the whispers behind their backs and saw fingers point when they came to town. Noah had left home to rid himself of the shame. After all these years, he realized he had allowed it to take hold of him, and no matter how far he traveled, he couldn't remove himself from the memories and the pain until he embraced his past, accepted his father for who he was and then worked to forgive him for the dysfunction he had caused in Noah and Seth's lives.

Regrettably, as much as Noah wanted to forgive his dad, he couldn't. The pain was still too real. Then he realized the truth about Ruthie.

For so long, he had felt stung by her rejection, yet being with her again made him realize he was the one at fault. He had left Ruthie. She couldn't forgive him because the pain of being abandoned was still so real to her. Plus, Noah had not only abandoned her, but also their child. Some wrongs could never be righted. Ruthie could never forgive him just as he could never forgive his father or himself.

EIGHT

By the time they arrived at the post office, Ruthie was feeling less unsettled. The few people they passed on the street had smiled and nodded in greeting. Mrs. Deitweiler was nowhere to be seen, and there was no sign of any tall man wearing black and sporting tattoos on his arm. The boys had regained their youthful enthusiasm, and even the sun peered through the overcast sky. Her earlier concern eased, and she smiled as Noah and the boys left her at the post office and headed to the library across the street.

She waved a farewell, although Simon and Andrew were focused on Noah, probably talking about computers and questioning how they operated. At least Noah glanced back and waved. Ruthie appreciated the attention he gave to her sons, but she remained all too aware of the man who wanted to do them harm.

Stepping into the post office, she was relieved to find only two people ahead of her in line. She waited patiently and approached the postmaster's window after the other customers had been helped.

Mr. Hardy was a kindly man who had managed the local post office for as long as she could remember. His smile was warm and welcoming. "Ruth Plank Eicher. It has been a long time. I wondered if you would be coming to town."

"It has taken me a while to get here."

"You've got a pile of mail that I've been saving. Did you bring a satchel?"

She glanced down at her small handbag. "I have only my purse."

"I'll get a big plastic bag from the back." He paused to stare into her eyes. "I'm sorry about the accident, Ruthie. You and the boys doing okay?"

"*Yah*, *danki*, Mr. Hardy. The farm is a challenge, but the boys are a big help."

"Your *datt* was a friend. I miss him. He was fortunate to have you as a daughter. You are a good woman."

Her cheeks burned. She nodded her thanks and waited quietly as he found a bag and filled it with her mail.

"Do you still want me to hold your mail here until you come to town again? Or we could set up delivery to your home."

"Can I let you know the next time I stop in?"

"Of course."

Ruthie's heart was heavy as she left the post office. Glancing into the bag, she wondered what all the official-looking envelopes meant. She had buried herself on the farm for the last two months and had allowed the bills to mount. Now she had more with which to deal. With so little ready cash, she had wanted to provide the daily needs for her children instead of paying off bills, many of which Ben had left unpaid.

Focused on her own financial situation, she failed to survey the surrounding area and suddenly heard footsteps sounding behind her. She stopped at the intersection and looked back. Her heart lurched at the sight of a tall man dressed in black. He stared at her through narrow eyes. The man on the mountain had covered his face with a stocking, so his features had been unrecognizable. Could this be the same man who had attacked her?

The light changed and she hurried across the street. She glanced back. The man started jogging toward her.

The library was just ahead, but she did not want the man anywhere near her boys. She spied a flower shop on the far side of the library and hoped she could find safety there. Surely the man would not do her harm when other people were around.

Increasing her pace, she hurried past the library and slipped into the shop.

The clerk looked up from arranging a bouquet of roses. "May I help you?"

"I—I just wanted to look at some of your potted plants."

Glancing out the window, Ruthie saw the man hurry past the storefront.

"Let me show you what I have," the clerk insisted. She motioned Ruthie to the rear of the store and pointed out a number of potted plants, each more beautiful than the last. The woman rambled on about how to care for the plants to keep them healthy and blooming.

Grateful though Ruthie was for having a place to hole up, she was eager to join Noah and her boys at the library and was relieved when a phone rang. The clerk excused herself and hurried to the far end of the counter to take the call.

Ruthie slipped outside and glanced along the sidewalk, seeing only a woman pushing a baby stroller. Letting out a sigh of relief that the man was gone, she hurried to the library and walked across the large stone portico. As she opened the door and stepped inside, someone bumped into her.

She glanced up. Her heart raced. The man in black. He must have backtracked to the library when the clerk showed her the potted plants.

The man's face twisted in recognition. "I thought I had lost you."

Her boys. Had he done anything to Simon and Andrew?

"What are you doing here?" she demanded.

"You dropped this."

She looked down at the letter in his outstretched hand.

"You need to be careful." He pointed to the bag she held close to her chest. "You wouldn't want to lose any more of your mail."

She took the letter, and before she could react, he was gone. She watched him run across the street and disappear into a wooded area not far from the post office.

Glancing down at the envelope, her breath hitched. The letter bore a stamp and had been mailed to her rural address. The script was the same as the writing on the notes she had received at home that demanded she leave the area, and all three missives had been written in the same shade of green ink.

Was he merely returning a letter she had dropped? Or was the man today the same person who had attacked her on the mountain?

Noah glanced at his watch, concerned about what was taking Ruthie so long. He should have waited for her at the post office until she got her mail. If the boys hadn't been so excited about visiting the library, he might have been more cautious.

He was ready to head outside to check on Ruthie's whereabouts, when she raced into the computer area, eyes wide and face flushed.

From her expression, he knew something had happened, and it wasn't good. "Stay here, boys. I want to talk to your mother."

Noah hurried to her side. "Are you all right?"

"A man dressed in black came after me."

"The same man from the mountain?"

"I am not sure. He gave me this envelope. He said I had dropped it." She was talking fast, the words spilling one after another out of her mouth.

"Calm down, Ruthie, and tell me you are all right."

She pulled in a breath and nodded. "He did nothing to harm me except make my heart nearly stop beating." She explained about him following her across the street.

"I dashed into a flower shop until he passed by. Then when I entered the library, he was there. Somehow he had doubled back. Perhaps when I was with the clerk in the rear of the store."

She held up the envelope. "He said I had dropped this letter."

"Did you see tattoos on his arm?"

"He wore a long-sleeve shirt." She shook her head. "Perhaps I am being foolish, but I feared he would grab me."

"Do you want to read the letter now?"

"Not now. I do not want the boys to know."

Noah understood. Ruthie always put her boys first. He admired her for that.

"Come, the boys are excited about the computer. We will focus on them now and deal with the man later. I called the sheriff's office. We can talk to one of the deputies this afternoon."

"I am not sure, Noah. What will the deputy say?"

"He'll say you need protection."

"My father never wanted to deal with the authorities. Neither did Ben."

"But you are wiser than your father and your husband.

Besides—" he glanced at where the boys sat in front of the computer "—you need to think of Simon and Andrew."

She nodded. "You are right. My safety is not as important as theirs."

"All of you are important, Ruthie. The man needs to be stopped."

He needed to be stopped now, before she was hurt again or he injured the boys. If anything happened to any of them, Noah wouldn't be able to forgive himself. He had made so many mistakes in the past, he couldn't make any more now that Ruthie and Simon and Andrew had come into his life.

NINE

Ruthie pulled in a deep breath to calm her pounding heart and racing pulse. She did not want the boys to suspect that she was upset. Andrew was still young and overlooked subtle nuances, but Simon had always been more attuned to her feelings. He could sense her upset even when she tried to appear calm. At the moment, she felt totally out of control.

Her concern was for naught. Both boys were so engrossed with the computers that they failed to notice anything different about her demeanor, for which she was grateful.

"This is cool," Simon enthused.

She did not know where Simon had learned about something being cool, but his statement was followed by laughter from Andrew.

Worried they were making too much of a ruckus, she patted both boys' shoulders and then held her finger to her lips. "*Shhh*. You need to be quiet."

Glancing at the large monitor, she shook her head. The bishop would not approve, of this Ruthie was certain, but when she leaned closer, she saw Bible verses printed on the screen.

Noah pointed to the lines of text. "I told the boys how the Bible can be accessed on the computer. We were looking up some of their favorite verses of Scripture."

Bible verses were not what she had expected to find on the screen. Once again, Noah had surprised her.

"What's your favorite text?" she asked, trying to keep her voice light in spite of her still erratic heartbeat coupled with her surprise at the boys' search for Scripture.

"Matthew 6:14 to 15." He pointed to Simon. "Look it up and read the verses to your *mamm*."

"I need to remember what you told us." Simon carefully tapped the keyboard.

"Now hit Enter," Noah prompted.

A new verse appeared on the monitor. Simon leaned closer. "The passage says, '*For if ye forgive men their trespasses, your heavenly Father will also forgive you. But if ye forgive not men their trespasses, neither will your Father forgive your trespasses.*'"

Ruthie was amazed at how easily Simon had pulled up the passage. She glanced at the text. Forgiveness sounded easy and it was the Amish way, but sometimes the results of one's mistakes caused too much pain. The act could be forgiven, but life would be forever changed.

"What about the man who plans to buy your property?" she asked Noah. "Did you find him on the computer?"

"Not Prescott Construction. He must not advertise on the web."

Ruthie pointed to the nearby youth section. "Boys, find a book to check out while I talk to Noah." Both Simon and Andrew hurried to the area designated for children.

"You are teaching the boys something they will never use," she said to Noah once they were alone.

"When they are older and want to get a job in town, Ruthie, they will need to use a computer. Many Amish craftsmen use computers to keep in touch with their customers and to order their supplies. As I understand the *Ordnung*, technology can't come into the home, but in an office or an outbuilding it's allowed for business purposes."

"Perhaps you are right, but for now, we are farmers who do not need technology."

"Let me do a little more searching while the boys find books to read, then we'll have lunch. I promised pizza if that's okay with you."

"Pizza would be a special treat."

Noah was exposing the boys to so many things. She would not let their minds be turned to the ways of the world, but for one day, allowing them to experience something new would be all right. At least, she hoped it would not cause them problems when they returned to the farm.

Ruthie's mind would be filled with other thoughts, as well. Would she be content to hole up on the mountain with no one around?

Prescott Construction. Would a construction company be her new neighbor after Noah left the mountain?

Perhaps by then, the bridge would have fallen into the water, isolating her even more. Her shoulders slumped with concern as she thought again of the man who wanted to do harm to her and her children.

She turned and stared at the other library patrons, searching for the man who had retrieved the dropped envelope to make sure he had left the library and had not returned. After what had happened, she never wanted to see him again, and she never wanted her sons to worry about a man who might attack their mother or bring harm to either of them.

"It's time for lunch," Noah said once they left the library. "I mentioned pizza earlier. Does that still sound good?"

"We like pizza," Simon said, serious as always.

Andrew tugged on Noah's hand. "Can we have pepperoni?"

"Whatever you want." He looked at Ruthie. "And whatever your mother says you can have."

"Pepperoni and peppers." Simon grabbed his mother's arm. "Please, *Mamm*."

"Yes to both, if Noah agrees. Anything sounds delicious to me."

On the way to lunch, they stopped to watch a train chugging through town. The boys were wide-eyed with excitement as the train whistle blew and the engineer waved a greeting.

"Someday I want to ride in a train," Andrew enthused.

"Yah." Simon nodded in agreement. "And I want to take that trip with you."

They were still talking about trains when Noah ushered them into the pizza parlor. "Table for four," he told the hostess.

"Family of four," she said into a microphone.

Noah swallowed down a lump of regret. If only they were a family. He had lost that chance ten years ago, when he had left Ruthie and his Amish faith.

A waitress hurried to help them and ushered them to a table.

The boys played word games printed on paper place mats while Ruthie watched.

Noah touched her arm. "Pepperoni and peppers?"

"The boys will love that."

"How about a second pizza with mushrooms and onions?"

She lowered her gaze.

"Isn't that what you liked years ago?"

She nodded. "You remembered."

"Why wouldn't I? We were close, Ruthie."

"Best friends growing up."

He smiled. "Along the way the friendship ended and something more developed."

She glanced at the boys, who seemed oblivious to their conversation.

"We are just talking about friendship," Noah assured her. "There's nothing to be concerned about."

Glancing over her shoulder, she studied the various customers already enjoying lunch. "I keep thinking about the man who followed me today."

"Do you see him here or anyone else who looks threatening?"

Trying not to be obvious, she peered at the people sitting around them. "There are a few men who are the same height, but no one looks like the man who followed me today."

Noah glanced at the corner table, where two men shared a pizza. Both were big and beefy and wore longsleeved black polos and khaki slacks. A logo was embossed over their shirt pockets, but Noah couldn't read the lettering.

He dipped his head toward the table. "Either of those guys look familiar?"

"One man seems in his fifties, the other is much younger. From their clothing, it appears they work together."

"Maybe Prescott Construction," Noah mused as if grasping for straws.

"I cannot read the logo on their shirts. You could ask them who they work for," Ruthie suggested.

He shook his head. "Not today. Besides, if they are with the construction company, I wouldn't want to do anything to sour the land deal."

"Of course not."

He heard sarcasm in her voice.

"Did you notice anyone with a tattoo?" he asked.

"Because of the cool temperature, everyone is wearing long sleeves."

"A description of the tattoo will help the sheriff find the attacker."

"I still do not want to discuss this with law enforcement."

"Law enforcement will find him," he assured Ruthie.

But would the sheriff's department find him before he came after Ruthie again?

TEN

"Thank you for bringing us to town and for all the ways you are making this day special for the boys," Ruthie said after the waitress had taken their order.

"The boys are special to me, Ruthie."

She glanced away, unwilling to meet his gaze.

He touched her arm again. "It's okay."

"You are selling your property."

He nodded. "I am."

The waitress filled water glasses for the adults and brought orange drinks for the boys. Two pizzas arrived soon thereafter. The boys ate until they were seemingly stuffed.

Ruthie laughed as she reached for her third slice. "This is more pizza than I've had in years," she confessed.

Noah smiled. "I'm glad. Pizza is always good. This seems especially so. We don't want any leftovers."

Simon and Andrew stepped up to the challenge and each boy ate two more slices. "I'm full," they both said in unison when they finished.

Noah glanced at the bag Ruthie had placed on the floor next to her chair. "Looks like you have a lot of mail to read."

"I should have come to town earlier."

"Have you talked to the post office about delivering mail to your house?"

The boys were once again engrossed in their place mats and laughing among themselves. Ruthie lowered her voice so they wouldn't hear. "The postmaster mentioned home delivery. Ben had arranged for them to hold the mail for his monthly trip to town."

"While you stayed on the mountain?" Noah asked.

She nodded. "I needed to stay to care for my father."

The waitress brought the check. "I'll pay at the register." Noah slipped from the chair.

Ruthie instructed the boys to wash their hands and faces in the restroom. She glanced again at the two men eating in the corner, realizing there was nothing familiar about either man except that they were tall and muscular.

As she looked around the pizza parlor, she saw a number of other patrons with similar builds. She had to stop seeing the man from the mountain every time a tall, bulky guy appeared. Men dressed in dark clothing seemed even more suspect to her.

She looked at Noah as he stood in line to pay the cashier. He fit the mold, as well. Tall and well built, he was wearing a long-sleeve navy blue shirt with dark trousers, yet she knew Noah would not do her harm. At least not physical harm. If she did not guard her heart, she would be hurt in unseen ways when he left. She did not want to get involved with any man again, especially Noah.

As soon as the boys returned to the table, she gathered her mail and handbag and followed them to the front of the pizza parlor.

A big man dressed in black with dark eyes and a scowl walked inside just as the boys neared the door. Simon nearly collided with him. Not the man who had stopped her at the library, but someone who gave her pause.

The guy grabbed her son's shoulders. "Watch where you're going, little man. You don't want to get hurt."

Something in the man's annoyed tone made Ruthie's stomach tighten. Everything happened so fast. He was standing in front of Simon one second and hurrying into the main dining area the next.

Wishing she had gotten a better view of his face, she grabbed both boys' hands and pulled them into a sitting area away from the door.

Simon frowned as if to say he was too old to hold his mother's hand. *"Mamm,"* he moaned.

She ignored his annoyance. "We'll wait here patiently for Noah before we go outside."

"I did not mean to get in that man's way," Simon said.

"Did he hurt you?"

Simon shook his head. "No, but he looked familiar."

"Could he have been the man you saw at the river's edge? The man who wanted to know where to fish?"

"I am not sure." He turned and looked into the dining area. "Where did he go?"

Ruthie glanced over her shoulder and studied the people sitting at various tables, but she did not see the big man with the dark gaze.

"Perhaps he went to the restroom," she suggested.

Noah paid the bill and joined them at the door. "Everything okay?"

Ruthie glanced again into the dining area. She was not convinced the man was in the restroom. Had he gone out a back door? If so, why had he passed through the pizza parlor? Was he here to spy on them?

"Ruthie?" Noah raised an eyebrow. "Is everything okay?"

"Yah," she said, unwilling to tell Noah about her concerns. "Everything is fine."

"The sheriff's office is on the next block," Noah said once they were outside. "We'll go there next."

"Thank you for lunch," Ruthie said.

He smiled. "I'm glad you enjoyed it."

"The boys did, as well." She gently nudged them.

Taking the hint, they both said, "Thank you for the pizza."

"We'll do it again, *yah*?" He patted their shoulders.

"Yah!" Smiles covered both boys' faces.

They skipped ahead on the sidewalk, giving Noah an opportunity to talk to Ruthie.

"You need to tell the sheriff's deputy everything that happened."

Her face grew serious. "I am not sure this is a wise idea. What can he do?"

"He knows people in town, Ruthie. He hears things. There may be a stranger causing problems. The deputy can question him and learn the truth."

She nodded. "If you think it will end the attacks, then I will talk to the deputy, although I do not know if he will listen to an Amish widow who lives so far from Willkommen."

"Too many Amish are wary of law enforcement, but the sheriff's deputies are not to be feared."

"I will follow your advice, Noah."

"Good." He glanced at the boys as they approached the upcoming intersection. "Turn left at the corner," he cautioned.

Ruthie hurried to catch up to them. She glanced over her shoulder a number of times until Noah looked back, as well.

"Something's bothering you," he said.

"I am thinking the boys are much too visible in case the attacker lives in town."

"I should have brought the buggy."

"The exercise is *gut*, but perhaps I am also worried about what to tell the deputy."

"Just tell him the truth."

"I would not lie." She squared her shoulders.

"I didn't say you would."

The boys glanced at each store-window display they passed, finding wonder in the items for sale. "It is so long since we have been to town," Andrew said. "There is so much to see."

Tires squealed around the corner and a dark sedan with tinted windows approached at a high speed. Noah quickly herded Ruthie and the boys away from the road. The car's front tire came up on the sidewalk.

Ruthie screamed and shoved the boys farther from the car. Noah turned as it raced past. He focused on the rear license plate, but mud was smeared on the plate and he was unable to read the numbers.

Ruthie grabbed Noah's hand. "If you had not moved us away from the curb, I fear what would have happened." Tears filled her eyes.

He wrapped his arm around her shoulder and then pulled the boys into his embrace, too. "The car's gone and we're all okay."

"But—"

He nodded to her, knowing there was a reason the car had jumped the curb, and it wasn't because the driver was going too fast. With the tinted windows, he couldn't see the driver's face, but he was sure the guy was the same man who had come after Ruthie. The attacker was in town at this moment. Noah didn't want to scare the boys more than they already were, which is what he tried to silently convey to Ruthie.

She wiped her eyes and nodded back to him as if understanding that she needed to be strong for the boys' benefit.

Noah glanced in the direction the car had gone. The guy who wanted Ruthie's property was becoming unhinged. One thing was certain—Ruthie and the boys were in his crosshairs.

ELEVEN

Coming to town had been a mistake. Ruthie knew it in the depths of her being. She clung to her boys. Her heart pounded almost as fast as the automobile had raced past them.

"*Mamm*, who was driving that car and why does he want to hurt us?"

Simon's question deserved an answer, but a lump filled her throat at the thought of what could have happened. Noah must have understood her upset. He patted Simon's shoulder.

"The man was driving too fast, Simon. Cars are dangerous, as we all know. We must be cautious, even on the sidewalk."

"I did not see the car until it had already passed," Andrew said. His little face was drawn and pale.

Noah nodded. "You boys responded immediately and stepped out of danger. That was very good."

Both boys seemed to take pride in their ability to react quickly. "That man should not be able to drive along the streets," Andrew said, staring in the direction the car had gone.

"If the sheriff had seen him," Simon said, "he would have gotten a ticket and his license would have been taken away." He looked up at Noah. "We need to tell the sheriff about what happened so he can arrest that man."

"We'll tell him, Simon. That's a good suggestion. The sheriff needs to know."

Ruthie's father had insisted the Amish take care of their own problems and not involve law enforcement. She had agreed to talk to someone at the sheriff's office, but she did not want to reveal family difficulties to a deputy she did not know. "I am not sure what we should do."

"Mamm!" Simon tugged on her arm. "You told me to be truthful when things happen even if I am at fault so I can learn from the mistakes. That man needs to learn from his mistakes."

She offered her son a weak smile. "How did you get so wise, Simon?"

He shrugged. "Perhaps it was the pizza."

In spite of the boy's serious expression, they all chuckled.

Ruthie turned to Noah. "Simon is right. We need to let law enforcement know about this driver and the harm he could cause."

The sheriff's office was located on the corner of the next block. She swallowed hard as Noah opened the door and motioned them inside. A bench sat on the right just inside the door.

"Boys, sit there while Noah and I talk to the clerk."

The man at the front desk beckoned them forward. Ruthie gave her name and address. "I need to report a number of things that have happened."

The clerk reached for a tablet and pen. "What type of things?"

"I received threatening notes that said I needed to leave the area or my children and I would be harmed. Then someone started a fire in my woodpile and attacked me when I raced outside to put out the fire. The man returned the next night. I believe the same person ran his car onto the curb not far from here and almost struck all of us."

The clerk wrote down the information she provided. "Could I speak to the sheriff?" she asked.

"He's out of town, but one of the deputies is available."

"That will be fine."

The clerk took the paper on which he had been writing and motioned them forward. "I'll take you to the deputy's office. There's a bench in the hallway where the boys can wait for you, if you like. You'll be able to see them."

She glanced at Noah, who nodded his approval.

"Mr. Schlabach will be with me. He is a neighbor and has witnessed everything I mentioned."

"That will be fine, ma'am. Step this way."

The clerk pointed to a bench for the boys and then ushered Ruthie and Noah into a small office directly across the hall. He gave the paper he carried to the man behind the desk. Ruthie looked back to ensure she could see the boys. They opened their library books and started to read.

The sheriff's deputy was middle-aged with a sagging jaw and warm gaze. He rose and stuck out his hand. "I'm Deputy Sam Warren."

Noah introduced himself and Ruthie.

"Please sit down, Mrs. Eicher and Mr. Schlabach. How can I help you folks?"

Ruthie went over everything she had told the clerk and then explained about the man who had questioned Simon near the river. She also mentioned the man at the library.

"Let's start with the person at the river. Can your son give a description of the man?" the deputy asked.

"Simon said the man was shadowed by overhanging branches so he could not see his face."

"What about you, Mrs. Eicher?"

"He wore a woman's stocking over his face. A knit

cap covered his hair. His eyes were dark, but that does not offer much help."

"Have you seen a doctor since the attack?"

She shook her head. "My bones did not break, so I will mend on my own."

"That's good to hear, ma'am. What about the boys?" He glanced into the hallway where the boys sat. "How are they doing?"

"They remain inquisitive about nature and the outdoors, but I am concerned for their safety."

"And, no doubt, your own safety, as well." He dropped his gaze to the paper the clerk had given him. "What about the car that ran onto the curb? Did either of you see the driver?"

Noah shook his head. "He drove a black sedan with tinted windows. I couldn't see the driver and tried to catch the license-plate number, but the plate was caked with mud and unreadable."

"Convenient for anyone who doesn't want to be identified," the deputy mused.

"We pushed the children out of the way," Ruthie explained. "If not—"

The thought of what could have happened returned to haunt her.

"Is there any other information you can provide about the man who attacked you that would be beneficial?" Deputy Warren asked.

"Tattoos."

The deputy picked up his pen. "What type and where on his body?"

"I do not know the type of tattoos." She pointed to her left arm. "His shirtsleeve came up at one point, and I saw the marks covering his skin from his wrist up."

"All the way up his arm?" Warren asked.

"I saw only as far as the shirtsleeve was raised. About midway to his elbow, so I cannot say about the rest of his arm."

"What about the colors of the tattoo and the design? Did anything stand out?"

"I feared he would strike me. I saw only the marks and nothing that I recognized."

"Tattoos that cover the entire arm are called sleeves, Mrs. Eicher. Often the various details in the design have a common theme. Did you see anything you could identify? And did he have tattoos on his other arm?"

"As I said, I do not recall seeing anything except swirls of color on his left arm. Yellow, red, blue." She shrugged. "I saw nothing on his right arm."

"Anything else?"

"As I mentioned, he was tall and muscular." She glanced at Noah. "Somewhat like Mr. Schlabach."

The deputy stared at Noah for a long moment. "What were you doing at the time of the attacks, Mr. Schlabach?"

"I was at my house just across the river from Mrs. Eicher's home."

"Did you see the suspect either time?"

"I saw a man dressed in dark clothing running from her house last night."

"You saw him from your house all the way across the river?"

Noah shook his head. "I had checked Mrs. Eicher's property and then decided to return to talk to her."

"About what, Mr. Schlabach?"

"Why did I want to talk to her again?" Noah asked.

The deputy nodded.

"To tell her not to worry."

"Yet the man was accosting her at that very moment."

Ruthie's stomach rolled. The deputy was implying Noah was involved.

"The door to her house was shut," Noah said. "I didn't realize what was occurring inside until I saw the door open and the man run away."

"Did you follow him?"

"No, I..." Noah glanced at her. "I was concerned about Mrs. Eicher's well-being and entered the house to check on her."

"I see." The deputy wrote something on the paper.

Ruthie glanced at Noah. His gaze was dark. He seemed as surprised by the deputy's line of questioning as she was.

The deputy pursed his lips and turned back to Ruthie. "Did you have the feeling at any time either night that Mr. Schlabach could be the attacker?"

She laughed nervously. "No. No thought like that entered my mind. Noah is an old friend who has helped me since he returned to the mountain. The other man is hateful. His heart is hardened and he needs to be stopped."

"Amish Mountain is a distance from town, Mrs. Eicher. If you were *Englisch*, I would advise you to call me as soon as you see anything that seems questionable, but I presume you do not have a phone."

"That is correct."

"Do you have access to a phone?"

She thought of Noah's cell. "For the next few days. After that time, I will have no means to communicate with your office."

"Living high on the mountain could be difficult, especially if the man returns to do you harm."

"*Yah*, I am all too aware of what could happen. That is why I need you to protect me."

"I'll have a car patrol the mountain each night, but I can't do more than that."

"Do you know of new people in town who fit his description?" she asked.

"Ma'am, the description you provided could fit a lot of men in town. Tall, muscular. Since he wore a stocking over his head, would you be able to recognize him in a lineup?"

She shook her head. "I saw someone in the pizza parlor and wondered if he could be the man, but it is too hard to know."

"You mentioned a man at the library."

"I had dropped a letter and he returned it to me."

"Was he tall and muscular?" the deputy asked.

She nodded. "And dressed in dark clothing."

"Did he have tattoos?"

"It is a cool day. He was wearing a long-sleeve shirt. I collected my mail at the post office and hurried toward the library." She explained about hiding in the florist shop and then bumping into the man when she entered the library. "After he gave me the dropped envelope, he hurried outside, crossed the street and went into the woods."

The deputy nodded. "There's a vagrant who set up camp in that area. We'll bring him in for questioning."

"Thank you."

"Could I see the envelope he gave you?"

"Two notes have been stuck under my door. Both were written in green ink and the script was the same as on the mailed envelope the man gave me today."

As Ruthie dug into the plastic bag of mail, the deputy asked, "Has the man given you any indication of why he wants to do you harm, Mrs. Eicher?"

"He wants me to leave my property." She told him what had been written on the first two notes and then held up the envelope in question. "The man who lives in the woods handed this to me."

Tearing open the flap, she glanced at the deputy and then pulled out the folded paper.

"Might be a good idea if I handle this one, ma'am." The deputy drew a plastic bag from a lower desk drawer along with a pair of tweezers. Using the tweezers, he opened the letter and read it, then placed it in the plastic and sealed it shut. "He's giving you until the end of the week."

"Does he say what he will do then?" Noah asked.

"He'll make you regret staying on the land." The deputy scratched his jaw. "Sounds as if he wants your property. Any idea why he wants your land, Mrs. Eicher?"

She shrugged. "The setting is lovely with a river that runs between my property and Noah's. Perhaps he wants a mountain home."

"Mr. Schlabach, the man has not come after you?" the deputy asked.

"I have received no threats or attacks to my person. Although a real-estate agent contacted me some weeks ago about selling my property. Prescott Construction is interested in the land."

"So both of you own mountain land that two different people or groups want?"

They nodded.

"Do you know about the movie studio that's on the other side of the mountain?" the deputy asked.

"I've only recently returned to town," Noah said. "Why would there be a movie studio in such a remote spot?"

"Low taxes. Pristine scenery."

"Could the movie-industry people want to film on the land?" Noah asked.

"Or perhaps build mountain homes for their executives," the deputy added. "I'll talk to the Montcliff Studio folks. We had some problems with them early on. Things have changed for the better." He shrugged. "Still, I'll let you know if I find out anything."

He turned to Ruthie. "Mrs. Eicher, if you see someone who looks like the man, let me know. There are a lot of new folks in town these days. Seems Willkommen is growing faster than anyone expected. New housing areas attract city people looking for a country home."

"Do you mean city people from Willkommen?" she asked.

He shook his head. "No, ma'am, from farther south. I was referring to Atlanta."

"They are moving to this area of Georgia?"

"'Fraid so. Our peace and quiet might be a thing of the past."

"Hopefully they will not come to the mountain."

"Looks like someone is already there stirring up trouble. Lock your doors and keep an eye on the boys when they're outside."

"You are scaring me, Deputy."

"Ma'am, I'm just speaking the truth."

Upon leaving the sheriff's office, Noah turned to Ruthie. "You don't look satisfied."

"I had hoped the deputy would know names and already have possible suspects in mind."

"Investigations take time, Ruthie. The deputy is trying to be realistic."

"Maybe I ask too much."

"To raise your boys in safety is not asking too much. You've filed a report so now the sheriff's office can act if they find someone questionable."

"I hope they find the man and lock him up," Simon said, overhearing their conversation.

"We don't wish harm to come to the man," Noah told the boy. "But we need to ensure he doesn't hurt anyone else."

"Just so he does not hurt my boys," Ruthie said. She glanced over her shoulder and tugged on Noah's arm.

He followed her gaze and saw a tall man in dark clothing. As Noah watched, the man turned the corner and disappeared from sight.

Ruthie was imagining that any tall, muscular man she saw was out to hurt her and her sons.

"Take a deep breath and try to relax," Noah suggested. "The deputy will be on the lookout for the assailant. You must be careful but not unduly paranoid."

She didn't seem interested in his advice.

"I need to stop at the lumber store for some building supplies," he explained. "Then we'll get ice cream before we leave town."

She studied the sky. "The clouds in the distance are as dark as my current mood. I am ready to head home, but I do not want to ruin the end of the day for the boys."

"The supply store won't take long. We'll be riding up the mountain within the hour."

She nodded as if satisfied with his answer.

"Climb in," Noah told the boys when they arrived back at the buggy.

He helped Ruthie to her seat and then scooted next to her. After a flick of the reins, Buttercup eased back onto the main street. The lumber store was on the south side of town. Ruthie kept her focus on the people and cars they passed, no doubt searching for her attacker.

Noah hated that Ruthie was living in fear, but her children were in danger, and she would do anything to keep them safe.

Once they arrived at the lumber store, Noah hopped to

the ground and tethered Buttercup to the hitching rail. "I won't be long if you want to stay in the buggy."

"We'll go with you," Ruthie replied quickly.

"I know you're worried about the boys, but from your frown, I also wonder if you're upset with me, Ruthie. Did I do something wrong?"

She shook her head. "You have been wonderful, Noah. I will never be able to thank you."

"The smiles on the boys' faces are thanks enough, though I would feel better if you smiled, as well."

She nodded. "Ben always said I was much too serious."

"And determined. You set your mind to something and you keep at it until you succeed."

"Things came more easily to you, Noah. I had to work for any skill or knowledge in school."

"Yet you made everything look easy, Ruthie."

They hurried into the lumber store and Noah found what he needed. After checking out, he loaded the items into the rear of the buggy.

Andrew tugged on Noah's hand. "Are we going to get you-know-what?"

Noah winked at Ruthie and then glanced down at Andrew. "I don't know what you-know-what is."

The boy motioned for him to bend down. "Let me whisper in your ear."

Noah enjoyed the game and stooped down.

Andrew cupped his small hand around Noah's ear and whispered, "Ice cream."

Straightening, he smiled. "That's a great idea. Do you think your mother and Simon want some, as well?"

Andrew nodded. He grabbed Simon's hand and whispered in his ear.

Simon's eyes twinkled and he nodded to Noah. "*Yah*, please. That sounds very *gut*."

"Are you boys keeping secrets from your mother?" Ruthie rolled her eyes, acting playfully indignant.

Andrew covered his mouth with his hand and giggled. "Close your eyes and we will take you there."

The boys guided her along the street and into the ice-cream shop, where she pretended to be surprised. Simon nodded to Noah and then motioned to Andrew, who was enjoying himself. Noah patted the older boy's back, proud of him for joining in and not spoiling his younger brother's fun.

From what he'd seen so far, Simon had a good heart and a sincere concern for others. Pride swelled within Noah, though he couldn't take credit for the boy. Ruthie had raised Simon. Her husband had, as well. Noah had done nothing for his child and couldn't even buy him a new hat and a better-fitting pair of shoes. At least he could buy him ice cream.

The boys ordered triple-scoop ice-cream cones with three different flavors and then tried to decide which they liked best.

"I like them all," Andrew said. He rapidly licked his cone as the ice cream melted.

Ruthie had one scoop of chocolate, and Noah splurged on two scoops of mint chocolate chip.

Once they finished the treat and wiped their hands and faces, they were ready to drive home. When they stepped outside, Noah eyed the dark clouds that hovered overhead and wished he had paid more attention to the weather instead of the fun he was having with Ruthie and her boys.

As he rounded the corner to the rear of the supply store, where he'd parked the buggy, Noah saw a man standing near the rig. A tall, muscular man wearing dark clothing.

The guy glanced at them, then turned and hurried down a back alley.

Ruthie was talking to the boys and hadn't noticed the man. Noah didn't want to worry her, but having someone snooping around the buggy was a concern. After the boys climbed in and he helped her to the seat, he checked his purchases from the lumber supply, relieved to find everything in place. Ruthie's mail looked undisturbed. He quickly inspected the wheels and the underside of the buggy. Nothing seemed amiss.

The stranger was probably walking through the parking area and had inadvertently passed close to Ruthie's buggy. Noah was making too much of something that was nothing more than happenstance. Plus, he didn't have time to track down the guy. From the dark clouds rolling overhead, they needed to start back to the mountain if they hoped to make it home before the rain.

TWELVE

Halfway up the mountain, the rain started to fall, fat drops that pounded the top of the buggy. A stiff wind drove the rain at an angle, drenching Ruthie and Noah. The boys got wet as well, even though they were hunkered down in the rear seat.

"Simon, make sure the bag of mail stays dry," Ruthie called back to him.

"The bag is plastic, *Mamm*. The envelopes are dry."

She grabbed blankets and wrapped them over the boys and then around her legs and Noah's.

The temperature dropped at least ten degrees, and the gusting mountain air and driving rain made the ride even more uncomfortable.

The buggy started to shimmy. Noah pulled back on the reins to slow Buttercup's pace.

Ruthie glanced around the outside of the rig. "The back rear wheel is wobbling."

Noah steered the mare to a clearing on the far side of the road. Before he could pull her to a stop, the wheel flew off and rolled down the incline.

The buggy shifted. Ruthie screamed.

"Hold on, boys," Noah warned as the buggy tilted, throwing Ruthie to the ground. The boys fell against the side of the buggy, then tumbled out, landing near their mother.

She screamed and crawled to her children. "Simon, Andrew. Oh, *Gott*, help us."

Heart in his throat, Noah jumped to the ground and hurried to check on both boys. They were stunned but sat up without a problem.

Tears ran from Ruthie's eyes as she gathered the boys into her arms. "I feared you both were hurt."

"Are you all right?" Noah kneeled beside her, touching her arms and legs to ensure nothing was broken.

"I am not so fragile to break in a fall."

Ruthie was strong-willed and determined, but her husband and father had died in a buggy accident. Noah knew the fear she had to have felt seeing her boys tumble from the buggy. His own heart had nearly stopped, too.

He led Ruthie and the boys to shelter under a large oak tree and wrapped the damp blankets around them. The rain continued as Noah retrieved the wheel and worked to reattach it to the buggy.

Noah thought of the man who had been snooping around the buggy. Loosening a few bolts could cause the wheel to shimmy off-kilter with time, which is probably what happened. When Noah had checked the wheels, all the bolts were in place, but evidently not screwed in tight enough.

He dug through the supplies he had purchased at the lumber-supply store and found bolts that would fit the wheel. He also found a toolbox in the rear of the buggy.

"You need help?"

Turning, he saw Simon, who had left the cover of the trees.

Noah appreciated the offer. "If you hold the wheel, Simon, I can slip the bolts in place."

Working together, they reattached the wheel. The mare would have to go slow, but they would be able to get home.

He helped Ruthie and Andrew into the rear of the buggy, where they would be at least somewhat protected from the rain.

"I will sit next to you," Simon announced.

"You'll be more comfortable in the back with your mother and brother," Noah encouraged.

"*Yah,* but it is good to be here with you."

Noah's less-than-thorough inspection of the buggy in town had placed Ruthie and her boys in a dangerous situation, yet he heard no accusation in Simon's tone, nor did he see anything except admiration in the boy's gaze.

In spite of the mistakes his biological father continued to make, Simon would grow into a fine man. Of this, Noah was certain.

Ruthie was too shaken to think of anything except that her boys had not been hurt. When she had seen them lying on the ground, she had thought the worst and her heart had been ready to break. Only two months ago, Ben and her father had been killed, although Ben's failure to stop at an intersection had placed him at fault. Still, no matter who was at fault, her husband and *datt* were dead, and today's accident had made her fear her boys had been injured.

With a grateful heart, she offered a prayer of thanks that her sons had been spared. Sensing Noah's upset, she tried to control her own emotions. She knew he held himself responsible, but he had done nothing wrong. No one would suspect someone would tamper with their buggy wheel. But someone had.

Again, she thought of the man in the pizza parlor, as well as the man who had tracked her down in the library. Could either of them be the man who had attacked her twice on her farm?

Hoping to keep Andrew warm, she wrapped him in her arms and pulled him close. Simon had to be chilled, but he was trying to be so grown up. Ever since Ben had died, he had considered himself the man of the house. Simon had taken on that role without her prompting, and she admired his internal sense of purpose, although she did not want him burdened with responsibility at such a young age.

Both boys were enamored of Noah, and as much as she enjoyed seeing them happy, she feared their spirits would be dashed when he left in a few days. To protect the boys she should stop Noah from coming around, yet she knew without a shadow of a doubt that Noah would do anything to keep them safe. With the hateful man on the loose, she and her sons were in danger, but knowing Noah was never far away provided a sense of security that would surely end when he sold his father's land and moved away.

Drawing Andrew even closer, she glanced down at the bag of mail and worried about what to expect tonight as she sorted through the bills. She would wait until the boys were in bed before she opened the envelopes, but the thought of what she might find unsettled her.

Tired and wet when they got home, she heated water on the stove and poured it into the washtub. Both boys bathed, enjoying the warm soak, then dressed in flannel pajamas.

After their filling lunch in town, Ruthie fixed peanut-butter sandwiches and wedges of cheese and apple for their evening meal.

Noah had parked the buggy in the barn, promising to work on the wheel later, and had gone home to change into dry clothes.

Her body ached, made worse by the cold. A hot bath would help ease the soreness, but by the time she tucked the boys in bed, the bath water had turned tepid, and she was too tired to refill the tub.

She washed her hands and face and changed into dry clothes. After throwing another log into the woodstove, she pulled her bent hickory rocker closer to the warmth and turned up the oil lamp.

Reaching into the plastic bag, she sorted through the mail. The flyers and pamphlets could be tossed, but she placed the important correspondence in a pile on the side table.

Her heart sank as the pile grew. She threw away the junk mail before she opened the bills, one after another. Her stomach churned as she realized how much debt Ben had accrued. He had cautioned her never to buy on credit, yet he had done that very thing more than a few times.

The fact he had taken out credit cards troubled her. She needed to talk to the bank manager the next time she went to town to see how much money was left in their small savings. She feared it was near rock-bottom, which only compounded her misery.

Overwhelmed with concern about her financial situation, she sighed before she reached for the next letter in her pile. The return address read Prescott Construction, the same buyer who was interested in Noah's farm. She ripped open the envelope and noted the letter had been written six weeks earlier and had probably been waiting for her at the post office all this time. The company expressed interest in buying her land.

As much as she wanted to keep her property and turn it over to the boys someday, she needed to be practical. If her financial situation was as dire as she believed it to be, she had to make some tough decisions. Selling the farm would break her heart, but taxes would soon be due on the land, and she needed money to buy feed for the livestock and seed for the fall crops. Money she did not have.

Was the offer from Prescott Construction the answer to her financial problems? She did not want to leave the mountain, but she might not have a choice.

Another thought surfaced that gave her pause. Could the man who wanted to do her harm be involved with Prescott Construction?

THIRTEEN

Noah returned to Ruthie's barn later that night to fix the broken wheel and soon saw her leave the house and walk to the graveyard. Despite the sweater she wore, she rubbed her arms against the cool evening air and paused at each grave, head bowed and shoulders slumped. Noah sensed the heaviness that appeared to weigh upon her heart. More than anything, he wanted to comfort her and apologize for not being more proactive today. Had he done a better job checking the buggy wheel, he could have had it professionally repaired before they left town. The ride home would have been wet but uneventful. Instead it had almost been a disaster.

As he watched, Ruthie kneeled on the damp earth and tugged at the weeds growing between the graves, no doubt wanting to ensure Ben's final resting spot wouldn't be blighted, as his life had been. The sight of such a caring and considerate woman mourning her husband with servitude wrenched his gut and brought a bitter lump to fill his throat. Ben didn't deserve Ruthie's love. Nor did Noah, yet she was too young to be a widow with two sons to raise by herself.

Her husband had been shunned, and Ruthie suffered with the shame. She had not been ostracized from the community, yet she had rejected any offer of help from the bishop and his church. Noah hoped that would change over time.

Eventually some handsome farmer would come courting. At first, he would help her with her farm. They would get to know each other until a bond formed that might eventually lead to love.

Ruthie was too pretty and sweet and hardworking to be ignored by the single Amish men in the area.

They were probably giving her an opportunity to mourn before they came knocking at her door.

Noah fisted his hands, surprised by the frustration mounting within him. Not at Ruthie, but at the men who would be vying for her hand. None of them would be good enough for her, but perhaps they could offer her what she wanted—to live Amish on her land.

Noah thought back over his years in the *Englisch* world. He had hoped life would be different when he left the mountain, but he had all too quickly learned that the internal struggle eating at him in his youth—his sense of inadequacy and need to isolate himself from his drunken father—remained constant.

He had also learned that the *Englisch* world, like the Amish, required hard work and steadfastness. He had done well with his jobs, and seeing Seth find love and have a family had brought him joy. Then the dam had collapsed and everyone he loved had been swept away.

Except Ruthie. She was the last link he had to the past. When he thought back to his youth, he had wonderful memories of their time together.

He continued to watch her as she pulled weeds and intermittently wiped at her eyes. Was she crying? Her tears broke his heart and confirmed she was not looking for anyone else to fill her husband's shoes. Even if Ben Eicher hadn't deserved her love and attention.

Glancing at the upstairs bedroom window, Noah wondered if Simon and Andrew were asleep. The boys were both so full of life and energy. The thought of them brought a smile to his lips and a joy to his heart that pushed past the pain of seeing Ruthie grieve for her deceased husband.

No matter how much Noah cared for the boys, he still needed to leave, so Ruthie could move on with her life. It wasn't what he wanted, but it needed to be done for her sake—for her future and that of the boys. Noah would only stand in the way of her happiness.

He turned back to the broken wheel, but his heart was heavy, and he decided to call it a day and return to his father's house. Things might seem better in the morning, although he doubted anything would be different. Ruthie would remain the dutiful wife grieving her husband's death, and Noah would be the man who had left her pregnant and alone. *Gott* help him for what he had done, even if he hadn't known about the baby growing within Ruthie's womb. Leaving her had been a huge mistake, and leaving his child compounded the guilt that welled up within him. Tonight, the pain of what he had lost was almost too much to bear. He needed to distance himself from Ruthie. She would continue to mourn her husband's passing while Noah mourned his youthful mistake that still ate at his heart.

After returning the tools to their rightful places, Noah peered from the barn to ensure Ruthie had gone inside. The now neatly weeded cemetery was empty except for the simple grave sites that marked the passing of her family.

Rain started to fall as he headed home. The river had continued to rise over the last few hours. If the water overflowed its banks, Ruthie's home could be flooded as had happened years ago when they were both children.

"She doesn't need any more problems, Lord."

Noah glanced back at her house, realizing that was the first time he had prayed aloud since the Chattanooga dam had broken.

Maybe he was starting to heal. Walking across the bridge, he shook his head at his moment of optimism. He would never heal, and that would be the burden he had to endure for the role he played in his brother's death.

Stopping on the far side of the bridge, he turned to stare at Ruthie's home, all the while ignoring the rain. As a kid, he'd enjoyed visiting his best friend, who eventually grew into the woman he loved. How had what started out so good turned so wrong? She had married someone else because Noah had thought of himself instead of what Ruthie needed.

Why hadn't he loved her enough to stay because he wanted her in his life? Some would argue that he was young and self-centered, both of which were true, yet he couldn't forgive himself for what he had done to Ruthie and, unknowingly, to Simon.

He turned back to his father's house and thought again of the lonely nights when his *datt* was drunk and ready to whip him for some imagined problem. Noah had never been good enough, but at least he had been the one his father punished instead of his younger brother. Seth had escaped their father's physical abuse, not that it made Noah feel any better right now.

Tonight, he felt once again like that boy going home to find his father either passed out in the house, or ready to take a strap to his backside.

Life back then had been tough, but that was the past and he needed to focus on the present. Being with Ruthie and the boys over the last few days had brought Noah joy, although he would leave soon. He didn't deserve happiness, and without Ruthie and the boys he would never be truly happy again.

Ruthie stood in the unlit downstairs of her house and stared out the window, watching Noah walk back across the bridge until he faded into the darkness.

Tired as she was, she hoped the night would be uneventful. The day had been a seesaw of emotions that had sapped her energy. Tonight she wanted to sleep without dreams of a man with a stocking over his head. She wanted to feel safe and secure in her own home without fearing what was going to happen next.

The deputy said he would have someone patrol the mountain. Would he be true to his word and would she even notice when law enforcement drove by? It was doubtful their occasional presence would deter anyone who wanted to do her harm.

She headed to the bent hickory rocking chair by the stove. After lighting the oil lamp, she reread the letter from Prescott Construction. If only she knew what to do.

Earlier, she had walked to the cemetery, where her mother and infant sister were buried, to draw strength and, hopefully, get answers.

Having her mother die in childbirth had rocked her world as a young girl. Her father had gone to get the midwife and told Ruthie to take care of *Mamm* while he was gone. He had returned soon after her mother had taken her last breath. Brokenhearted, Ruthie held on to the last words her mother had whispered on her deathbed. "Take care of your father."

Ruthie had tried. That was why she had not run away with Noah that night, much as she had wanted to. She had planned to talk to her father and soften the blow of her leaving, and work out some arrangement for his care.

All those plans were for naught because Noah had left without her, never realizing how he had broken her heart.

She laid the letter from the construction company on the kitchen table, turned off the lamp and slowly climbed the stairs to her bedroom. Once again, she pulled back the curtain and stared at the farmhouse on the opposite side of the river. A light glowed in a downstairs window.

She imagined Noah with a cup of coffee in hand, staring pensively back at her. How had their lives become so mixed up when they had been so much in love?

Some things were never meant to be, and perhaps she and Noah had never been meant for each other.

That realization made her heart ache as she crawled into bed and closed her eyes. All she could see was Noah's handsome face and his eyes twinkling with laughter as they used to do when they were both young and in love.

FOURTEEN

Noah couldn't sleep. He kept thinking of the buggy accident and what could have happened.

The rain increased through the night. Concerned about the rising river, he donned a water-repellant windbreaker, grabbed his Maglite and walked to the water's edge. The river churned as it flowed down the mountain, the current strong with whitecaps. If the river overflowed its banks, nothing would remain in its path.

He played the light over the bridge, checking the underpinnings, and realized he had not shored up the rotting wooden beams as he had planned to do. Tomorrow the bridge would be his first priority.

To ensure the muddy bank on Ruthie's side of the river was holding firm, Noah crossed the bridge. A noise sounded in the night. He flicked off the Maglite and made his way carefully along the river's edge. As he neared Ruthie's house and outbuildings, the sound came again, metal against metal.

Drawing closer, he saw movement.

Thunder rumbled overhead, then a bolt of lightning crashed to the earth. For a split second, he saw a man running from the chicken coop.

Noah raced after him. Another bolt of lightning struck. A tree cracked and branches crashed to the ground.

The man disappeared into the woods behind Ruthie's house.

Thunder roared and lightning once again brightened the night sky.

Noah ran to the chicken coop. As he drew closer, he realized the sound he had heard was the wire fence being cut. Some of the chickens had already escaped through the gaping hole that would allow a fox or coyote to attack those that remained behind.

His heart skipped as he thought about what the man might do next, and what could befall Ruthie and her boys.

Ruthie woke when a giant bolt of lightning struck nearby. She sat up with a start, hearing the raging storm. Concerned by the howling wind and torrential rain, she slid from bed, peered through the window and saw Noah. Hurriedly, she slipped on her robe, glanced into the boys' room to ensure they were asleep and then raced downstairs. Like a strobe light, the sky flashed bright, then dark, then bright again.

She opened the door as another bolt of lightning lit the sky and glanced at the chicken coop. Her heart pounded. Even from this distance, she could see the cut fencing and the chickens scattered about the side yard. There was another burst of light and she gasped.

Spray-painted on the wall of the chicken coop were the words *Leave now.*

"Mamm?" She turned to find Simon on the stairs.

"Go back to bed. It is only a storm, Simon. We are not in danger."

Turning back, she watched Noah wrangle the chickens into the henhouse. He grabbed tools from the barn and quickly closed the gaping hole before he hurried to the porch.

"You saw the coop?" Noah asked as he shook water from his jacket.

She nodded, then glanced over her shoulder, relieved her son had complied with her request. "Simon has gone back upstairs, but I fear he may have seen it, as well. Who would do this?"

"I saw someone running, but I couldn't catch up to him."

Her shoulders slumped and she was overcome with discouragement. "Maybe I should sell the farm."

"What?"

"Come in. I will show you the letter I received from Prescott Construction. I wanted to pass the land on to the boys, but so many bills came in the mail we picked up today. I am tired of trying to make ends meet while fighting off the vile man who wants me gone."

"You don't have to make a decision tonight, Ruthie."

She appreciated the concern evident in Noah's voice, but she had her back to the wall, figuratively, and needed a way to support her boys.

"I should return to town and talk to the real-estate agent about Prescott Construction's interest in my land," she admitted.

"We'll go together. I have to take the buggy to the repair shop. What I did tonight was a quick fix, but I don't want you going up and down the mountain without an expert checking the wheel."

"Could we go tomorrow?"

He nodded. "But first thing in the morning, I need to work on the bridge. We'll leave after that."

"I do not want the boys to know about selling the farm. At least, not yet. Once I find out what arrangements the company is willing to make, then I will know whether this is something I should do."

She glanced out the window. "When the rain lets up, I have to remove the writing from the chicken house. The boys have gone through so much. They do not need to worry more about their mother."

"I'll take care of it, Ruthie. There's spray paint in my dad's garage. I'll cover the writing. It won't look attractive, but we can buy paint in town. I'll repaint the structure and repair the wire."

Confused as to what to do, she wrapped her arms around her waist and sighed. "I do not want to give in to this man. If he wants me to leave, perhaps I *should* stay."

"To prove to him that he can't run you off?"

"Exactly. If my well-being was all I had to worry about, I would sink in my heels and remain here, but I worry about the boys. I have been schooling them at home, yet the needs of the farm are great and there is little time for lessons. I see them falling behind with their studies. In town, they could go to school with the other children."

"You love the mountain, Ruthie."

She smiled weakly. "Whether you realize it or not, so did you, Noah, but you left. This has not been a problem, *yah*?"

"I wouldn't be truthful if I told you it was always easy."

"Have you thought of returning to the Amish life?"

"At times."

"Yet something holds you back?" she asked.

"I never felt that I fit in. Perhaps it was because of my *datt*. Drunks are not living life according to the *Ordnung*. The district looked askance at my father. They also looked askance at Seth and me."

"You did nothing wrong."

"Perhaps I was too thin-skinned. The *Englisch* world taught me to be more independent and not worry about what others thought."

She nodded. "I should learn the same from you."

"You're not comfortable in town?"

"Perhaps I am too thin-skinned, as you mentioned."

"You were always well liked. Although because of your husband, I'm sure these last few years have been difficult."

"Things change, as we both know." She sighed and then pointed to the kitchen. "Shall I fix tea, or would you prefer coffee? Plus, I have a feeling you did not eat after our trip to town. I have cheese and bread."

"I'm fine, and the chicken coop needs attention. The boys rise early. It's best if I paint over the message tonight."

"It is still raining."

"And it may continue all night. You might hear me outside. Don't be alarmed. Lock your door and stay inside. I'll see you in the morning."

He had to be tired. They had both had a long day. His clothes were wet, and the weather was growing even more severe.

"You have done so much for me, Noah. I do not know how to thank you."

"Letting me spend time with you and Simon and Andrew brings me joy, Ruthie. For this, I should thank you." He started for the door, then hesitated and glanced back. "I'm sorry how everything turned out. I was impetuous and bullheaded. I should have thought of your needs instead of only my own."

With a nod of farewell, he strode out of the house and hurried toward the bridge. She locked the door and climbed the stairs. From her bedroom window, she watched when he returned and spray-painted over the vile message.

Once the job was done, he glanced up, no doubt seeing her in the window. He raised his hand and then hurried back across the bridge.

Shortly thereafter, lights came on in his family home.

As a girl, she used to stare out her window and think of a time when Noah would court her and ask to marry her. In her mind, it would have been the normal progression after all the years they had grown up together.

She turned away from the window, remembering how many nights she had cried herself to sleep after Noah had left the mountain. Her heart had broken, and at the time, she had feared she would not have the wherewithal to continue on.

Then came the realization that new life grew within her. For all her heartache, Ruthie had vowed to move on with her life for the sake of her child. She did not have Noah with her, but she had his child, and she would do everything to ensure that child was loved and embraced totally.

Then Ben had entered her life. He had sweet-talked her and put on his best behavior. Not long after their wedding, his true personality surfaced. By then, there was no going back, and once again, she had tried to make a life for herself and her baby. Not the life she had envisioned growing up with Noah, but a life that would provide a home for her son nonetheless.

Yet without a father's love, that home had never felt whole. With Noah back just for a few days, everything felt good and solid and filled with mutual support, though she needed to remember that Noah had left the faith and was no longer Amish, which meant there was no future for them together.

She feared getting hurt again when Noah left for a second time. Worse than her own pain was the fact that her boys would suffer, too.

Perhaps Noah should leave now before he became even more a part of their lives. But he had already worked his way into their hearts. She saw it in the boys' enthusiasm when they were with Noah, and she knew it when she was with him, as well. It was too late to put up her guard. Noah already had a place in her heart. Truth be told, he had always had one, even if they could never be together because of their differing faiths.

Another thought gripped her heart. When Noah left, she would be alone without anyone to help her protect her sons. The hateful man was determined to drive her off the mountain.

With Noah gone, she feared he would succeed.

FIFTEEN

Morning came early and brought clear skies, which was a welcome relief. Noah downed a cup of coffee, loaded his truck with lumber and headed to the bridge. Before long, he heard his name and glanced up to see Simon and Andrew running toward him. He laughed at their excitement.

"Did you tell your *mamm* you would be at the bridge?"

"She said to ask if you wanted our help. If so, we can stay. Otherwise she said we need to do our chores."

Ruthie stood on the porch of her house. He waved to let her know the boys had made it to the bridge and would be staying to help. The work went quickly. He enjoyed Andrew's chatter and Simon's tempered comments when his younger brother got too rambunctious.

Once the bridge was stabilized, Noah loaded his tools in the truck and told the guys to hop in the passenger side. He rewarded their hard work with moon pies that they gobbled down and then wiped their face and hands on his handkerchief before they drove to the barn and unloaded the rest of the wood there.

"Let's get the animals fed. Your *mamm* will call us soon for breakfast."

"She said we will not have eggs this morning," Andrew informed him. "*Mamm* thinks the storms and some kind of varmint upset the chickens."

Ruthie was right, but the varmint wasn't a fox or coyote. It was a two-legged kind.

"Maybe we can go to town and buy some more chicks that do not get spooked in the night," Simon suggested.

"Are we going back to town?" Andrew's eyes grew wide. "Twice in one week?"

Noah held up his hands. "You boys are getting ahead of me. I'm not sure when we'll go back to town, but no matter when we go, we need to ask your *mamm* about buying chicks before we jump to any conclusions."

"I hope she says we can go soon," Andrew said, "because I like eggs."

With three of them working, the chores didn't take long. Noah marveled at the boys' willingness to work and the weight they carried. Ben must have instilled a good work ethic in the boys. Or, more likely, it was due to Ruthie's mothering. Either way, Noah appreciated the fine young boys who were eager to pull more than their fair share of the load.

Ruthie called them for breakfast, so they washed at the pump and hurried inside.

Andrew inhaled the savory aroma when they entered the kitchen. "Are we having bacon for breakfast?"

Ruthie smiled. "Biscuits and sausage gravy."

"Yum! Next to eggs, that is my favorite."

Simon rolled his eyes and gave his younger brother a playful shove. "You like everything *Mamm* fixes."

"*Yah*, and I like what Noah fixes, too."

Ruthie gripped a large wooden spoon and pointed it at her sons. "Did I see you boys eating moon pies?" she asked, her eyes twinkling with amusement.

They stood still with hung heads and looked guilty.

Noah laughed. "That's my fault. I keep them in my truck. Simon and Andrew worked so hard on the bridge they needed nourishment."

She lowered the spoon and laughed as she hugged the

boys. "Moon pies are not necessarily nutritious, but they are good."

"They're yummy, *Mamm*."

"You look like you want another one, Andrew," she said with a chuckle.

"I could eat five of them."

"Well, instead of moon pies, we will enjoy breakfast. Fill Simon's glass with milk, then open a new bottle to fill yours, Andrew."

She pointed to the cabinet. "Simon, get the plates and carry them to the table."

"What can I do?" Noah asked.

"Would you mind pouring coffee?"

"My pleasure."

Her cheeks pinked. The bruise on her face had faded, and she had a lightness in her step that he hadn't noticed yesterday.

Maybe it was because the rain had stopped and the sun was shining. Noah's mood was upbeat, as well.

"Why does the chicken coop have black paint on one side?" Simon asked, staring through the window.

"I had some paint at my house and wanted to see if your mother thought the coop would look better painted black."

The explanation seemed to satisfy the boy.

"I like red better," Andrew said.

"Then we can get red paint in town, along with some chickens."

"I am not sure we need more chickens." Ruthie raised an eyebrow.

"But we want eggs," Andrew reminded her.

"Yes, we do," Ruthie agreed with her son. "We can buy a dozen or two at the store."

"Are we going to town today?" Andrew asked after he had poured the milk.

"Noah and I need to run some errands. I thought you boys might want to visit with Aunt Mattie."

"It has been a long time since we saw her," Simon said as he arranged the plates on the table.

"Do I know Mattie?" Noah asked.

"My mother's baby sister. She moved to the area the year Simon was born."

"You and the boys don't see her often?" he asked.

"She was out of town when we buried Ben and my *datt*. A few weeks later, she left a card and brownies on the porch asking me when she could visit, but I was not ready for visitors."

Noah understood. After her husband's death, Ruthie was hesitant to allow people back into her life. Even a loving aunt.

"Aunt Mattie will not recognize you boys as tall as you've grown," she said, smiling at her sons.

"The last time we visited, she made chocolate-chip cookies and homemade ice cream," Simon informed Noah.

Andrew rubbed his stomach. "The cookies were good, but the ice cream was delicious."

"Mattie's house is not too far outside of town," Ruthie said. "We can stop there first. As long as she agrees, you boys could help her with the chores while Noah and I run our errands."

"If you drive the buggy, Ruthie, the boys and I can follow you in the pickup. That way we can leave the rig overnight at the repair shop in town, if need be."

"They will enjoy riding with you, Noah."

Eager for another adventure, Simon and Andrew ate breakfast and finished the chores, then climbed in the pickup with Noah.

"I'm still concerned about the wheel," Noah told Ruthie, "so hold Buttercup to a slow trot. The boys and I will be right behind you."

He rolled down the windows and led them in singing church songs he remembered from his childhood as they followed the buggy down the mountain.

Mattie's house sat along a farm road about three miles from town. Ruthie pulled Buttercup to a stop in the driveway and seemed a bit nervous when she climbed down from the buggy and motioned the boys forward. Before they stepped onto the porch, the front door opened and a grey-haired Amish woman stepped outside, clapping her hands with joy.

"It has been too long." She opened her arms and hugged them all at once.

Andrew tried to wiggle out of her embrace. Simon glanced over his shoulder and rolled his eyes at Noah.

"Ruth Ann, you have been too long away from me," Mattie said. "It warms my heart to see you again and—" She stepped back to look at all of them. "And these boys have grown so big. You must come inside. I have cookies."

Andrew's eyes widened. "Aunt Mattie, the last time we were here you made ice cream."

"I remember, Andrew. Would you like to do that again? I'll need help turning the churn."

He held up his arm and showed his muscle. "I am strong."

"I know you are, and Simon is, as well. We can make lots of ice cream."

Ruthie touched her aunt's arm. "Mattie, this is Noah Schlabach. His family lived in the house across the river from us."

Mattie smiled. "I have heard about you, Noah. It is nice to meet you at last. You will come in for coffee and cake."

"And ice cream," Andrew added. "Right, Aunt Mattie?"

"Andrew," Ruthie chastised. "You are being much too insistent. Where are your manners?"

"I am sorry, *Mamm*. I must have left my manners at home."

"He is a wonderful boy." Aunt Mattie beamed. "Just as Simon is, and we will make ice cream in a bit."

"A cup of coffee and cake sound wonderful, Mattie, but we cannot stay long. We need to go to the real-estate office in town. Noah is selling his father's land."

"So many are selling their property."

"Amish farmers?" he asked.

"*Yah*, north of town a large development is being built. The bishop is not happy with the growth. He fears we will lose our peaceful way of life."

"In the past, there was nothing north of town," Ruthie said.

"So true, my dear, but things change. I wonder if they will start a new development on the mountain."

"Why do you say that?" Ruthie asked.

"You mentioned someone is buying Noah's property. It sounds as if homes will be built there, as well." She shook her head and tsked. "Too much growth too fast is never good."

Noah thought of his father's land and Ruthie's being divided into small lots dotted with homes that would mar the landscape. Did the man want Ruthie to flee from the mountain so he could have access to her land? How dark the man's heart must be if he would ruin a woman's life for his own personal gain.

A troubling thought caused Noah to flinch. Just like Ruthie's attacker, Noah had been thinking only of himself when he had left Ruthie ten years ago. Although she had continued on without him, Noah would never be able to forgive himself for causing her pain.

"Take your time in town and enjoy this beautiful day." Aunt Mattie stood on the porch with Andrew and Simon as Ruthie and Noah prepared to leave. "The boys and I will have ice cream waiting for you."

Ruthie regretted her own self-imposed estrangement from her aunt. After Ben had been shunned, she had become more reclusive and had only visited her aunt a few times in the last five years. Mattie had understood and had not barged in on Ruthie's privacy.

Today her greeting had been warm and sincere. Now that Ben was gone, Ruthie needed to visit more often. Being with her aunt would lift her own spirits and bring joy to the boys, as well.

Noah followed Ruthie to the buggy shop in town. Ivan Keim, a beefy Amish man with a ruddy complexion, owned the shop and agreed to check the wheel.

"I have three large jobs ahead of yours so I will not get to it for a day or two," he said. "You can board your horse at the stable in back. Unhitch your buggy and leave it here. My son will help you with your mare."

Once Buttercup was taken care of, Noah held the passenger door for Ruthie and helped her into his pickup truck.

"I have not ridden in such a vehicle before, Noah. This is an adventure, as the boys would say."

He laughed. "They wanted to sing songs on the way to Mattie's house. Did you hear us?"

"I heard nothing except the clip-clop of Buttercup's hooves on the pavement."

"Next time, we'll sing louder."

"A singing when we get home tonight might be fun."

He nodded. "I'm sure the boys will enjoy showing off their talent."

"But I do not want them to be prideful, Noah."

"I don't think you'll ever have that problem with Andrew or Simon. They are hard workers and considerate boys who will grow into fine men."

"Someday they will marry and give me grandchildren. This is my hope."

"Simon is not yet ten, Ruthie." His eyes twinkled playfully. "Aren't you moving a little fast?"

She laughed. "*Yah*, I want them to remain young, but I also think of children in the future who will carry on the family name."

"The Eicher name?" The buoyancy in Noah's tone faltered.

"At least their last name is not Plank," she countered.

"Meaning you married Ben so Simon would have a surname other than your own."

She could not bear to look at Noah. What he said was true, but she had been too caustic with her words. Had she wanted to cause him pain, the same way he had hurt her long ago? That was not what *Gott* would want her to do. She must ask forgiveness for her disregard of Noah's feelings. She must also wipe the hurt from her memory so it would not fester again.

"I would like to take back my words." She hung her head and was unsettled with remorse.

"I'm sure it was hard for you to be pregnant without a husband."

"I was not as concerned for myself as I was for my child, but that time has passed. I should not look back."

"I'm sorry, Ruthie."

"It is over. We will speak no more about what happened."

"It's not over if you're still hurt by what happened."

She turned to gaze into his eyes. "Some pain leaves quickly, like a stubbed toe or a hangnail. Other pain lasts a lifetime." She glanced out the window again. "I accept your apology. I hope you will accept mine. We do not need to mention this again."

He hesitated for a long moment, then said, "On a different note, I like your aunt."

Ruthie nodded as she adjusted her seat belt. "Mattie is a *gut* woman."

"She obviously enjoyed seeing you and the boys again."

Her sweet aunt did not harbor any ill will toward Ruthie, and she had never chastised her for marrying Ben. The problem was in Ruthie's mind, not Mattie's.

"Let's talk to Deputy Warren first and then we can stop at the real-estate office," Noah suggested. "Hopefully Vince Ashcroft will be there today."

"I hope he will know if Prescott Construction is still interested in my land. As I told you, I have a stack of bills that must be paid."

"You could take out a loan and pay it back little by little."

"Which would only place me deeper in debt."

"You wanted to pass the farm on to the boys," he said, as if she did not remember her reason for holding on to the land.

"I still do, Noah, but I have to use my head as well as my heart. My heart tells me to remain on the farm. It has been my home for twenty-seven years, but my head reminds me that if I cannot pay my bills I could lose everything, including my farm."

"I can help you, Ruthie."

She held up her hand to stop him from saying anything more about her financial situation. Although she appreciated his offer, she would never be able to live with herself if she accepted his pity or his money.

"I am not sure what I will do with the land, but one thing is certain. I will not let that terrible man on the mountain take anything that belongs to me."

She pursed her lips before continuing. "Talking to the real-estate agent will provide information that might help me make a decision."

Noah sighed. "I hate to think of you leaving the mountain when the boys seem to love it there."

"You loved the mountain, Noah, yet you left."

"I thought we weren't going to talk about the past?"

She nodded. "My mistake."

Shame on her for returning to the very subject she had said was off-limits. What was wrong with her these days? When she was around Noah, her mind played tricks on her. At some moments, she saw herself as a young woman starting out in life with the man she loved.

Letting out a sigh, she shook her head. The thought was so unsettling, thinking of where they both were now. One *Englisch*. One Amish.

"Is something wrong?" he asked.

Glancing out the passenger window, she tried to act as if she was not concerned about anything, when in reality her heart was heavy. The man on the mountain was a constant worry and threat to her own well-being and her children's, but the bigger threat was Noah. The longer she was around him, the more comfortable she became. How could she separate herself from the memories of the past? Being with him brought everything to the forefront and made her realize what she had lost when Noah had walked away. She should have run after him, but she did not know where he had gone. If only he had come back.

But he did come back, a voice bubbled up within her.

The voice was right. Noah had come back, but he was ten years too late. Even more unsettling, he had left his Amish faith and had come back *Englisch*!

Perhaps she had been foolish ten years ago to believe they would have remained committed to the Amish way if they had left the mountain together. She liked to think her influence would have kept Noah Amish. Now she could do nothing to change his mind about the life he had chosen to live.

Amish and *Englisch* did not mix, as much as she wished it was not so.

SIXTEEN

As they drove through town, Ruthie studied the people, looking for tall, muscular men with tattoos on their left arms. She did not see many tattoos, but she did see a number of big, bulky guys who could easily be the man who had come after her on the mountain. If only she could remember something else about his clothing or appearance.

Noah pulled out his cell. "I'll call the sheriff's department to ensure Deputy Warren is in his office." He tapped in the number, asked to speak to the deputy and then paused.

"I'll check back later." He disconnected and glanced at her. "Deputy Warren is at city hall with the mayor. He should return in an hour or so. We can stop by then and tell him what happened last night."

Ruthie wanted to know if the deputy had made any arrests. She was being optimistic, but she wanted the attacker apprehended and locked behind bars.

Noah braked the truck to a stop at the red light. He pointed toward the appliance store on the corner, and Ruthie followed his gaze. A large-screen television sat in one of the windows.

A commercial caught their attention. A big man dressed in a plaid suit stepped on-screen and gestured toward a billboard behind him. The sign read Your Home's a Castle with Castle Homes!

Noah groaned.

"What's wrong?" Ruthie asked.

"That's Floyd Castle. He used the same line in Tennessee."

"You know him?"

"Only by reputation. Seth bought one of his homes." Noah explained about the dam's collapse and Seth's death along with his family.

"Oh, Noah." She grabbed his arm. "I am sorry."

"It was my fault."

She shook her head. "How can you say such nonsense? You had nothing to do with the dam collapsing."

"I'm the one who told Seth about the development and the discount given to those who worked on the bridge."

"You did not know what would happen."

"I encouraged Seth to leave home even though our *datt* never laid a hand on him. Seth didn't get into trouble, but he came with me because we were a team, two kids always trying to outsmart their father."

"You were the older son, Noah. Your father was angry about life. He took that anger out on you."

"He was ashamed of himself, Ruthie. That shame ate at him and led him to drink. When he drank he saw himself as someone else, someone better or more successful. The sad thing is that down deep, I truly believe my father was a good man. If only he could have realized he had worth and that people would accept him for who he was."

"He changed when your mother died. My father did as well, when my own mother passed."

Noah nodded. She saw the regret in his eyes.

"The woman is the heart of the family," Noah said. "When the heart is gone, the body dies. My father didn't want to live without my mother, and he made it difficult for his children."

She could relate. "We had similar backgrounds. Perhaps that is why we became so close."

"It was more than our families." He turned to stare at her.

Ruthie's breath hitched. She glanced away, unwilling to lose herself to the memory of what they had had so long ago.

The light changed to green. Noah turned left and headed along the side street. There were railroad tracks ahead, and the lights were flashing.

"Looks like we'll be stopped by the train."

She smiled, glad to have something else to fill her thoughts. "The boys never tire of watching them pass."

The crossing guardrail on the opposite side of the street lowered, but the one on their side failed to engage.

"Something's wrong," Noah said as he pulled the pickup to a stop.

The roar of the approaching train filled the air, and the earth beneath them vibrated.

Seemingly concerned about the broken guardrail, Noah glanced in the rearview mirror and frowned. Ruthie looked back. A red truck pulled up right behind them. As the train neared, the truck inched closer.

"I'm not sure what that guy's doing," Noah said, his voice tight with worry.

The red truck tapped their rear bumper, pushing the pickup forward.

Ruthie gasped.

Just that fast, the truck tapped them again, sending them onto the tracks.

The train's deafening whistle blew. The engine loomed over them. Ruthie braced for impact and screamed.

Noah floored the accelerator and steered around the working guardrail to the other side of the tracks.

Time stopped for one long moment before Ruthie realized they had escaped without a collision.

Heart in her throat, she looked over her shoulder and watched the train race through the intersection. The truck that had rear-ended them turned around and dashed away.

"Oh, Noah, we were almost killed," Ruthie gasped. Tears filled her eyes and her hands trembled. "What happened?"

"We were shoved in front of the train by someone who wanted to do us harm."

"The man from the mountain." She dropped her head in her hands. "When will it end?"

Everything had escalated in that moment. Being pushed in front of an oncoming train ratcheted up the danger even more. Before this, the man on the mountain had wanted Ruthie to leave her land. Now he wanted her dead.

Noah steered his pickup to the side of the road and braked to a stop, then reached for Ruthie and pulled her into his arms. Her face was pale and she was shaking.

"It's okay, Ruthie. Neither of us was hurt."

"The train came so close. It was the man on the mountain. His attacks are getting deadly."

He held her until her trembling eased.

"Take a deep breath. The danger has passed."

"Yet the outcome could have been so different, Noah."

The man needed to be stopped, but they had to determine who he was first. Once they notified the sheriff's office, the deputies would be on the lookout for the red truck. Even with law enforcement's help, Noah still needed to be vigilant to ensure nothing else happened to Ruthie.

She pulled in a deep breath and eased out of his arms.

"Do you know anyone who drives a red truck?" he asked, relieved to see color return to her cheeks.

She shook her head. "The people I know drive buggies."

"I couldn't see the license plate. I'll call the deputy sheriff and tell him."

The deputy was still out of the office. Noah told the clerk about the driver of the truck obviously trying to do them harm. "Tell all your deputies to be on the lookout," Noah said. "This guy has got to be stopped. He's getting more aggressive and he means business."

"We'll find him, sir. You can be assured of that."

Noah wasn't so optimistic.

"You do not look satisfied with law enforcement," Ruthie said after he had disconnected.

"They don't seem to be as involved as I would like them to be."

"I am Amish, Noah, and I live on the mountain. As I mentioned to you before, out of sight, out of mind."

"Maybe, although I hate to think that would be the case. We'll talk to Deputy Warren this afternoon when he returns to his office. Hopefully, he'll be more concerned about your situation."

"What about talking to the real-estate agent?"

"I'll call them now."

He tapped in the number and the receptionist answered on the third ring. "Ashcroft Real Estate, Tiffany speaking."

"This is Noah Schlabach. I stopped by yesterday in hopes of talking to Vince Ashcroft. Is he available today?"

"Mr. Ashcroft should be in his office after lunch."

"One o'clock?" Noah asked.

"Closer to one thirty."

"Are the papers ready for the sale of my land?"

"Could you refresh my memory, sir?"

Noah let out a frustrated sigh. After the train incident, he had run out of patience. "I have a home and acreage on Amish Mountain. Prescott Construction made an offer on my property."

"That's right. I remember. I'm sorry, but I don't have information about the offer, sir. You'll have to talk to Mr. Ashcroft."

"Do you have a point of contact for the construction company?"

"I didn't see a name on the initial correspondence."

"Schedule me for one thirty," Noah said.

"Could you repeat your name?"

"I could and I will." He glanced at Ruthie and shook his head. "Noah Schlabach. Shall I spell my last name?"

"No, sir. I've got you down for a one-thirty appointment with Mr. Ashcroft."

"Thank you, Tiffany."

He disconnected. "If Tiffany is any indication about how Ashcroft Real Estate operates, we might be dealing with the wrong real-estate agent."

"Hopefully, Mr. Ashcroft has information on Prescott Construction. Perhaps if I decide to sell my land and move to town, the boys and I would be safer."

Noah wouldn't dissuade Ruthie from doing what she thought was best for her family, but he wanted her attacker stopped. Now.

"I could apply for a job as the real-estate agent's receptionist," she added. Her lips tugged into a brief smile, which relieved him even more.

"Can you use a computer?" he gently teased.

She nudged his arm. "You know I cannot, which only proves your point about the boys yesterday. You might be right, Noah. Simon and Andrew will need to get jobs when they are older, especially if we live in town. Computer skills are necessary, even for the Amish."

"You can still follow the *Ordnung* within your home. No computers, no televisions, no technology in the house."

"'No fun,' the boys would say, once they are exposed to the ways of the world."

"You might underestimate them. I lived in the world for the last ten years, yet I still see the good in living Amish."

She tilted her head. "But I thought you were ready to leave the mountain?"

He was, yet when he was with Ruthie thoughts of settling down and embracing his Amish roots took hold of him like a dog tugging at his pant leg.

Looking away, he shook his head. "I'm not sure what I want."

"Sometimes it is hard to know. Have you asked *Gott*?"

"He and I have been somewhat estranged."

"Maybe it is time to get to know each other again."

"You might be right." He squeezed her hand. "Do you feel up to a visit to Mountain Bank? It's not far from here."

"I want to ask them about my account, so, yes, stopping there will be fine."

Noah drove the few blocks to the bank and pulled into the parking lot at the side of the large stone structure. "Let's talk to the bank manager. He might know something about Prescott Construction."

Before they reached the entrance, two men barged out of the bank. One was a portly man wearing a plaid suit. Noah recognized Floyd Castle and tapped Ruthie's arm to get her attention.

The other man was tall and muscular. He wore a long-sleeve black shirt and khaki pants. "We saw him at the pizza parlor," Ruthie said, her voice low. "He was sitting with another man in the rear of the restaurant."

Castle pulled at his collar. "Look, Burkholder, I don't care what kind of problems you're having. You sold me on the idea of a lake and said you could make it happen. Now you're making excuses."

"The deal's taking longer than I expected."

"That's your problem, not mine."

Both men hurried to a white sedan with dark windows. The man called Burkholder took the wheel, and the sedan pulled onto the main road, heading north.

"We need to find out who Burkholder is," Noah suggested. "Someone who works at the home-development site, for sure."

"Castle did not seem happy."

"Nor did Burkholder. Looks like there might be trouble with Castle Homes."

They hurried inside and asked to speak to the manager. The receptionist led them to a small office, where a bald man in his midforties stood to greet them. He stuck out his hand. "George Masters. How can I help you folks?"

Noah introduced himself and Ruthie, and explained that they lived on the mountain and were considering selling their properties. "Prescott Construction has made an offer on my land. Vince Ashcroft notified me of their interest. He's been out of town, but I'm hoping to meet with him later this afternoon. I'd like to know who I'm dealing with and thought you might have information about the construction company."

The manager tugged on his jaw as he thought for a moment. "That's not a local firm. Of course, we've got a lot of folks passing through town these days. Let me check my computer."

He tapped his keyboard and stared at his monitor. "They haven't done business with us or they would be in our system. But that name sounds familiar."

"I thought the same thing and did a computer search but came up with nothing."

"Wish I could help. I do know there's a lot of interest in new property these days. The mountain would seem like prime real estate, especially for someone, maybe from the movie studio, wanting to build a getaway retreat. I don't want to talk out of turn, but there are two real-estate companies in town. Willkommen Realty is an established firm. They're reputable and well thought of by the local townspeople and business owners."

"Are you saying there might be a problem with Ashcroft Real Estate?"

The manager shrugged. "I'm not saying anything except Vince came to town not long ago. I wouldn't want you to get involved with someone who was less than reputable."

Ruthie scooted closer in her seat. "Mr. Ashcroft is not reputable?"

Masters spread his hands. "I'm just telling you he's new and inexperienced."

"I appreciate your honesty," Noah said. "We saw a Castle Homes commercial on television. He must be building in the local area."

"North of town. Ashcroft Real Estate is handling the sales. Got himself on Mr. Castle's good side." Masters shook his head. "I'm not sure how, although it should be a gold mine for him if he plays his cards right."

Noah looked at Ruthie. She raised an eyebrow. "Mr. Ashcroft likes to gamble?" she asked.

The banker smiled. "He's gambling on Castle Homes drawing people from other parts of the state. I'm not as confident about the attraction."

"You don't think buyers will want to move to the North Georgia mountains?" Noah asked.

"Some folks will, but he's planning on three building phases of one hundred homes each. That's a lot of newcomers to town. The bank will enjoy opening new accounts, but I've got to tell you, this town will be hard-pressed to take care of that many folks, especially if they move in within a short period of time. A lot of the locals are worried. I tried to tell Castle to go slow, but he's got these grand ideas about making a fortune. He's dealing with another bank in town, though he stopped by to see if I could offer him a better loan, which I couldn't."

"He's been successful in other areas of the country," Noah said.

Masters nodded. "True, but his company was nearly wiped out with what happened in the Chattanooga area. Not sure if you read the papers, but a dam broke and his housing development was flooded. Folks died. Houses that hadn't sold were washed away. Castle had insurance but not enough to cover his losses."

"My brother and his family were in one of those homes, Mr. Masters."

"I'm mighty sorry. A tragedy, for sure."

"Why did Castle choose Willkommen for his next housing project?"

"Land was relatively inexpensive here compared to the big cities. The way I see it, he wants to turn his company around and thought this would be an easy sell. He rushed in without doing enough homework."

Noah was interested. "What do you mean?"

"His community is centered on a man-made lake. Somewhere he got the idea he could feed it with a natural spring, only there's no such thing in that area. He cut down the vegetation and ended up with a dust bowl that is less than inviting. Ask anyone in town. They'll tell you the same thing."

"We saw him outside your bank in a heated conversation with another man."

"Probably Brian Burkholder, his foreman. From what I gather, Burkholder claimed if they dug a lake, he could ensure it would fill by the grand opening next week. Even with this current rain, the lake is less than one-third filled. People don't want to see a mud hole when they are looking at possible home sites."

"Sales aren't going well?" Noah asked.

Masters shrugged. "He's tight-lipped about everything, but that's what I hear."

The bank manager drummed his fingers on his desk. "Anything else I can help you folks with today?"

"Could you check my bank account?" Ruthie asked. "My husband kept track of our finances. He died recently, and I want to ensure the balance in the checkbook is accurate. The only identification I brought is the bank statement. I hope that is sufficient." Ruthie handed him a statement that included her account number.

"That will be fine, Mrs. Eicher, and I'm sorry about your loss." He typed the account number she provided into his computer. "Ruth Ann Plank Eicher?"

"That is correct."

"I knew your dad. He often talked about his daughter who cared for him."

Ruthie's eyes widened. "Did he bank here?"

"No, ma'am. You might want to check North Georgia Bank."

He tapped the keyboard. The printer hummed. He pulled the paper from the machine and handed her the printout. She studied the information before folding the paper and tucking it in her purse.

Noah leaned forward. "Could you check to see if my

father had an account?" He provided his father's name and his own driver's license for identification.

"Reuben was a customer." Masters typed something into the computer and nodded. "You're on his account." The banker handed Noah the printout.

"I'll leave the money in the bank for now, but after the land sells, I might decide to close the account."

"Whatever you decide works for us."

"Thanks for your help." Noah stood and shook the banker's hand.

"Good seeing you both."

Noah hurried Ruthie to his truck. "Let's see if Vince Ashcroft is in his office. I'm interested in what he has to say about our properties. Plus, I want to know why all of a sudden someone wants to buy land on Amish Mountain."

Noah felt like he was in the middle of a giant jigsaw puzzle. He had a number of pieces, but none of them fit together. One thing was certain, the land was secondary compared to Ruthie and her boys. His first priority was to keep them safe.

SEVENTEEN

Noah parked in the rear of the real-estate office. He opened the passenger door and escorted Ruthie inside. The receptionist he had met yesterday smiled. "Mr. Schlabach, right?"

He nodded and introduced Ruthie. "Is Mr. Ashcroft available?"

"He just arrived. I'll tell him you're here." She slipped from behind her desk, hurried down the hall and entered an office, closing the door behind her.

Not more than thirty seconds later, she returned. "Mr. Ashcroft would be happy to see you now."

The real-estate agent stood as they entered his office. He extended his hand and offered them a wide smile and a limp handshake.

Vince Ashcroft was pushing fifty with a receding hairline and bushy eyebrows. A small tuft of facial hair protruded below his lower lip and looked like a smudge of dirt on his otherwise clean-shaven face.

"Sit down and we'll discuss the contract from Prescott Construction." He tapped on his keyboard and then studied his monitor. "You've got the Amish Mountain property on the north side of the river."

"That's correct." Noah nodded. "I'd like to know the construction company's offer and how soon we can close the deal."

"Didn't I mail that information to you?"

"I never received anything."

Again Ashcroft tapped his keyboard. His printer hummed into operation. He pulled a piece of paper from the machine. "Here's the offer they're making." He pointed to the amount with his pen.

"I don't know what property is going for around here," Noah admitted, "but that seems low."

Very low, plus Noah was less than satisfied with Ashcroft claiming he had sent papers Noah had never received.

"If you had land in town, I'd say you were right. But Amish Mountain is a different ballgame, so to speak. We don't have any comparable sales in that area. You could counter."

Noah sighed. "I had hoped everything could be wrapped up quickly."

"And it will be if you decide to accept their offer. As long as their funding comes through, we could have the sale completed by the end of the week."

"Let me think it over."

"Certainly, although they might find another property if you drag your feet too long."

Noah didn't want to be pushed into accepting a low bid. "Do you have any idea why they're interested in the land?"

"As I mentioned, Prescott Construction contacted me by email. You'll find their email and mailing addresses on the printout I gave you. We haven't discussed anything over the phone."

"Do you have their number and a point of contact?"

"Ah…" Ashcroft hesitated. "Let me check the computer." He studied the monitor and scrolled through a few pages. "Hmm? Strange. We don't have a point of contact or a phone number for them."

"That seems unusual."

"It's an out-of-state company…" The agent shrugged. "Some people like to keep their anonymity."

"And when they do," Noah said, feeling even more unsettled, "I always wonder why."

"I own the neighboring property," Ruthie interjected. "Prescott Construction contacted me by mail and expressed interest in my land, as well. Have they mentioned acquiring my farm?"

Ashcroft shrugged. "They haven't mentioned any other land, but I could email the company."

The agent glanced at Ruthie. "Do you want to sell?"

She held up her hand. "I am interested in finding out how much they are willing to spend. Depending on their offer, I would decide whether to sell or not."

"You farm the land?" Ashcroft asked.

"That is correct."

"With your husband?"

"My husband passed away two months ago."

"I'm sorry for your loss, but I can certainly understand your desire to move off the mountain."

"I do not want to move, Mr. Ashcroft, but I am making inquiries."

"I see. How many acres?"

"Fifty-five."

"Nice. I'm sure I can find a buyer for you." He made a note on his tablet and then asked, "What about the mortgage?"

"It is through a local bank."

"Without any lends or other loans attached to the farm?"

"That is correct."

The agent nodded. "I'll email Prescott Construction and see what they say about your property."

"Thank you, Mr. Ashcroft."

"Of course." He glanced at his watch. "I hate to cut this short, but I have a meeting to attend. Is there anything else I can help you with?"

"How long before the papers would be ready to sign if I accept the offer on my land?" Noah asked.

"Two or three days, tops. Call my receptionist when you come to a decision."

"Cell service on the mountain is hit-or-miss. I'll stop by your office in the next few days."

"I'll see you then." Ashcroft rounded his desk, shook their hands and then opened his office door. "Good talking with you, folks. I'll be in touch."

As they stepped into the hallway, Noah spied a poster advertising Castle Homes' grand opening next week.

"This is a new development in town?" he asked the receptionist, hoping to get more information.

"Yes, sir. It's located about five miles north of Willkommen. Take Wagner Road and you'll see the signs for the office. There's a model home to tour if you're interested."

"Someone's out there now?"

She nodded. "The office is open until five thirty."

"Thanks, Tiffany."

"No problem. I almost forgot, I just received something from Prescott Construction. On the phone, you asked about a point of contact. Brian Burkholder's name is on the offer."

"He works for Mr. Castle?"

She shrugged. "I don't know about that, but I saw his name on the papers."

"You've been a great help, Tiffany."

She smiled. "Ashcroft Real Estate aims to please."

As they left the real-estate office, Noah leaned closer to Ruthie. "Did you get the idea Ashcroft wanted us out of his hair or was it my imagination?"

"After what the banker said, I wonder if he is a reputable agent, Noah. I would not want his inability to broker a deal to impact the sale of your father's land."

"I've got a strange feeling about Ashcroft, as well as Prescott Construction. I smell something fishy and we're quite a distance from the river."

They hurried toward his truck.

"Let's check out Castle Homes," Noah suggested. "I want to see what Floyd Castle is up to. He wheels and deals, and I don't like fast-talkers who always want to make a quick buck. Plus, I want to learn more about Brian Burkholder."

Noah checked his watch when they climbed into the truck. "Bottom line, I don't trust Castle. His foreman might also be questionable."

Before Noah turned the key in the ignition, a car raced out of the real-estate parking lot and turned north. A small sports car. Vince Ashcroft sat behind the wheel.

"Our real-estate agent seems to be in a hurry," Ruthie said.

Noah nodded.

Ashcroft had gotten flustered when Noah asked for Prescott Construction's phone number. The real-estate agent was being less than forthright. He knew more than he wanted to let on and that worried Noah. What was Ashcroft hiding, and who really wanted to buy the mountain land?

"Can we stop at the sheriff's office before we visit Castle Homes?" Ruthie asked. "The deputy may have information about the red truck that pushed us onto the train tracks. Plus, I want to find out about the man who lives in the woods. The deputy said they would bring him in for questioning. I need to know what they learned."

Noah checked his watch. "Deputy Warren should be in his office, which isn't far from here."

After a series of turns, Noah parked on the street in front of the sheriff's office and ushered Ruthie inside.

The clerk smiled in recognition. "You folks here to talk to Deputy Warren? He's at his desk. Go on back."

The deputy was as welcoming as he had been the day prior. "How are the boys?" he asked.

"They're making ice cream with my aunt Mattie."

"Such fine lads." The deputy pursed his lips. "I understand you had another incident in town."

Noah explained about his pickup being shoved onto the tracks as the oncoming train neared.

"Did you see the driver?"

"Unfortunately the windows were tinted. I called your office after it happened and talked to the clerk," Noah said. "I doubt it was a coincidence since so many things have been occurring. Someone's trying to frighten Mrs. Eicher."

"And they are succeeding," she admitted.

"The dispatcher relayed the information about the red truck to the deputies on patrol. No one has seen the truck, but we'll continue to be on the lookout."

"You'll let us know if you locate the truck and the driver?" Noah asked.

"Definitely. Have any other problems developed?"

"The man returned last night." Ruthie explained about the cut chicken coop and the threat spray-painted on the henhouse.

"One of our patrol cars was up there around nine p.m. before the storm hit. He didn't see anything amiss."

"What about the movie studio?" Noah asked.

"The head of the studio met with the mayor this morning. I spoke with the studio director following their meeting. He's working hard to ensure a good partnership with the townspeople and was concerned to hear about violence on the mountain. He'll have his security team on the lookout for anyone matching your description."

"Did you mention the tattoos on the man's arm?" Ruthie asked.

"I did. In the past, we didn't see many heavily tattooed folks in town, but that's changed over time, and even more so since the movie studio moved to the area. The head of the studio assured me his security folks will question anyone who seems suspect, and he'll call me if they uncover anything."

"Their cell coverage must be better than mine," Noah mused.

"They put up a tower to solve that problem. You're situated on the wrong side of the mountain."

"Evidently."

"What about the man who has been living in the woods?" Ruthie asked.

"The one who returned your dropped envelope?"

"*Yah*, did you get a chance to question him?"

"We searched the woods, but he had cleared out of his campsite and was gone. Those transient types don't hang around long, especially when they know they're not welcome."

"Maybe he headed back up Amish Mountain," she mused.

"Give us time, Mrs. Eicher. We'll find your attacker and take him into custody."

Noah explained about overhearing the argument between Castle and Burkholder. He also mentioned that the receptionist in the real-estate office claimed Burkholder was part of Prescott Construction.

"Well, isn't that interesting." The deputy pulled on his

jaw. "Does Burkholder want your land for his own personal reasons, or is he acting as a front for Mr. Castle?"

"That's what I've been wondering," Noah admitted.

"Either way, you folks need to let us handle this from here on out. Don't mess where you're not wanted. You've already got one man coming after you, Mrs. Eicher. I wouldn't want anyone else to get upset with either of you. We'll do our job and let you know what we uncover."

Ruthie's spirits were low when they left the sheriff's office. She had hoped the man in the woods was the same man who had accosted her. She wanted him locked up and not able to hurt her or her boys. The deputy said to give law enforcement time, but Ruthie didn't have time if the man came after her again.

EIGHTEEN

Noah and Ruthie left town and headed north on Wagner Road. The two-lane paved highway meandered through a forested area of tall pines and sturdy hardwoods. Rounding a bend, they came to the foot of a narrow valley that had been cleared of vegetation. Wind whipped down from the mountain, blowing dirt and debris.

"This looks like the middle of the desert instead of the Georgia mountains," Ruthie said as she eyed the naked land.

"They've removed the trees and destroyed the vegetation," Noah said. "Then they'll charge new home owners additional fees to landscape their property."

Signs pointed them to the home office. Noah pulled into the parking lot. "Let's see if we can find someone who can show us around."

No sooner had they climbed from the truck than a tall, lanky guy, in his late twenties with red hair, wearing a black polo and khaki slacks, hurried from the office to greet them. *Castle Homes* was embossed over the pocket on his shirt.

Ruthie eyed the logo as he neared. "Brian Burkholder and the other man we saw at the pizza parlor wore the same shirts."

"I'm Dave Herschberger." He shook Noah's hand and nodded to Ruthie. "You folks looking to buy a home?"

"We stopped at the real-estate office in town," Noah explained, "and saw a poster for the development."

"Yes, sir. We'll have three hundred homes by the time all phases of the project are completed." He pointed to the office. "You'll find maps and brochures inside. Also, an artist's rendering of the entire area."

"How long before you're built out?" Noah asked.

"That depends on sales. The homes are moving fast so we anticipate twenty-four months to have the first phase completed."

"You bought Amish farms?" Ruthie asked.

"Some of the land belonged to the Amish. Other pieces of property belonged to regular folks." He nodded to Ruthie. "No offense, ma'am. I guess you call us fancy. Mr. Castle pays top dollar. His offers were too good to pass up."

"Seeing your last name, I wonder if you were raised Amish?" she asked.

"No, ma'am. Fact is my last name's Hersch. Mr. Castle likes us to use Amish names so we fit in with the local folks. I don't think it has much bearing on people from Atlanta coming to buy a new home, but from what I heard, it helped convince some of the Amish farmers to sell their land."

"Yet Mr. Castle did not change his name," Ruthie said.

"No, ma'am. But then everyone knows Mr. Castle."

"Did you work with Mr. Castle on his Tennessee housing development?" Noah asked.

"No, sir. I'm from Georgia and started working for him a month ago."

"By any chance, do you know anything about Prescott Construction?"

The guy shook his head. "Doesn't sound familiar. I

could call our building foreman if you'd like. He might know of the company."

"Brian Burkholder?"

"That's right. Do you know him?"

"I've just heard the name." Although Noah would like information about why Burkholder and Prescott Construction wanted land on Amish Mountain.

Dave pointed to the office. "Let's go inside and get a cool drink while I show you the brochures."

Noah didn't want a cool drink, but he wanted to see Castle's concept for the development.

The air-conditioning was on in the trailer and the thermostat was set low. Ruthie rubbed her arms when she stepped inside.

A three-legged easel held a large poster board with a drawing of the final housing development. The town of Willkommen could be seen to the south of the site, with Amish Mountain in the distance to the west.

Noah stepped closer, noticing a large central area colored blue. "Is that a lake?"

"Yes, sir. That's one of the main drawing cards for our development. A two-hundred-acre man-made lake, perfect for fishing or boating. A beach will be on the eastern edge with picnic grounds. Plus, there's a playground, pool and tennis courts nearby."

"The developer thought of everything."

"'Your home is your castle—'" Dave began, reciting the builder's motto.

"'In a Castle home,'" Noah interrupted, finishing for him.

The guy smiled and handed both of them brochures. "There's a map of the home sites. Why don't you folks take a look around?"

"You mentioned calling your foreman about Prescott Construction."

"That's right." He tapped a number into his phone, waited for a moment and then shook his head. "He's not answering. I'll contact John Zimmerman. He's the assistant foreman."

This time the call connected. "John, I've got a couple interested customers here at the office who will be looking around the site. One of them wondered if you knew anything about Prescott Construction." The redhead nodded. "I see." He smiled at Noah. "I'll tell him." Another pause. "That's right."

Dave disconnected and stuck his phone in his pocket. "John knows of the company. Evidently someone took it over not too long ago. Prescott Construction is headquartered in Tennessee."

"Did the assistant foreman work on Mr. Castle's home development near Chattanooga?"

"No, sir. He came onboard when this project was in the early stages. I've heard him talk about the dam in Chattanooga a few times so he might have worked on the dam but not Castle's housing project."

Noah's neck tingled. "How was he involved?"

"Seems he mentioned the concrete supplier."

The concrete that had failed to hold. Whether it was poorly designed or poorly constructed would take a long time for the inspectors to determine. Until their investigation was final, Noah was suspicious of anyone tied to the dam.

He tried to place the assistant foreman. "What's Zimmerman look like?"

Dave shrugged. "About my height. Brown hair." He glanced at a poster on the wall. "There's a photo of both the foreman and the assistant foreman."

Noah and Ruthie moved closer. "He was the man we saw eating pizza with Brian Burkholder," she said to Noah.

He nodded. The two guys sitting in the corner.

Both men were tall with dark hair and dressed in the same Castle uniform that Dave wore. Standing in the foreground was Vince Ashcroft. The real-estate agent was shaking hands with Floyd Castle.

Noah leaned in closer and read the names identifying each person. Assistant foreman John Zimmerman and foreman Brian Burkholder.

Everyone used a German last name. Noah motioned Dave closer. "You're telling me the foreman's name is really Brian Burk."

The man smiled sheepishly, as if realizing he had said too much. "Ah, no, sir. The foreman's last name is really Burkholder."

"What about Zimmerman? Is his real name Zimmer?"

Dave laughed nervously. "Look, it may sound strange, but Mr. Castle knows the little things that make a difference when you're purchasing land. What can I say?"

He had already said too much. Bottom line—Castle couldn't be trusted. If his workers used false names to fit in with the local Amish, no telling what else he would do to see his development succeed. Although how this site north of town had anything to do with either Noah's land or Ruthie's property was the question Noah couldn't answer, yet everything pointed to a connection.

Noah put his hand on the small of Ruthie's back and guided her toward the door. "Why don't we look around outside?"

Dave hurried after them. "Wait, folks. I'll give you my card."

He grabbed a business card from a nearby desk and

handed it to Noah. "We've got a home offer for you." Glancing at Ruthie, he added, "And you, too, ma'am.

"Stop back after you drive around," Dave continued. "We can go over some numbers. The model home's open next door. Be sure to check it out. You'll enjoy all the comforts of a Castle home."

Noah knew the comforts that could be washed away in a wall of water all too well.

Once Ruthie and Noah stepped outside, she said, "Dave seems a bit aggressive to me."

"He's repeating all of Mr. Castle's phrases. Castle's the one who seems to be moving fast and going in big for this area of North Georgia."

"I hate to think what will happen when all these people move to Willkommen. It makes me glad I live on the mountain."

"Let's drive around the site. Maybe we can get a different perspective on what's going on here."

The streets were marked, but only a few were paved. From the sizes of the lots, the houses would be close together with little green space.

Stopping at the top of a hill in the rear of the development, Noah pointed to Amish Mountain in the distance. "Notice anything up there?"

They both got out and walked to the edge of the road. Ruthie held her hand over her eyes to shield the sun's glare. "Is that my house?"

"Between the trees. I can see the waterfall farther up the mountain and the river that forms at the bottom of the falls, and then runs down the mountain, passing between our farms."

She stared at the mountain and nodded. "Your house is barely visible to the right of the river. I never realized a natural valley leads down the mountain toward this area."

"Because the river turns at the junction of our properties and flows along the southern valley to the other side of town. That's where we always focus."

"Ever since seeing the rendering of the lake, I keep wondering where Castle plans to get the water." She turned to Noah, her face drawn. "Looks like they could get it from the river with just a little engineering. Lowering your side of the riverbank and damming up my side would redirect the water down the northern valley."

Noah nodded. "Then Castle has his lake."

"So how's Prescott Construction involved?"

"Brian Burkholder is the common thread that ties everything together." Noah hesitated for a moment and then added, "What if Prescott Construction or Brian Burkholder doesn't want Castle to succeed? Castle may not know who's behind Prescott Construction."

"Or, does Prescott Construction want our land so Burkholder can up the price and sell it to Mr. Castle for a profit?" Ruthie added.

"Maybe, especially if he and Castle have some negative history from their days in Tennessee."

"I do not like any of this, Noah."

They climbed back into his pickup and started down the hill. As they rounded one of the sharp curves, a dump truck filled with gravel raced around the bend and headed straight toward them.

Ruthie screamed.

Noah turned the wheel. His pickup swerved out of the way just in time. Gravel flew from the top of the truck and pummeled his pickup, nicking his windshield.

"That was intentional," Noah said as he strained to catch sight of the driver.

Ruthie patted her chest as if to calm her heart. Her eyes were wide, her mouth drawn.

"Are you okay?" he asked, seeing her ashen face.

"I saw the man driving the truck." She grabbed his hand. "Oh, Noah, he had a stocking pulled over his face just like the man who attacked me on the mountain."

Ruthie's heart continued to pound at an erratic rate. The near miss had scared her. Seeing the man behind the wheel of the dump truck had scared her even more.

The man on the mountain who had attacked her wore a stocking pulled over his face. From the distorted features of the man driving the truck today, he had to have pulled a stocking over his face in the same way. She could not describe his features, yet everything within her had shuddered when she saw him. Her inner voice of warning screamed that the mountain attacker was after her again.

"A feeling came over me that it was the same man." She hugged her arms around her, hoping to ease the inner tension that wound her tight as a spring. "Then I realized he was wearing a stocking. It is more than a coincidence, Noah. He has to be the same man."

"We'll stop at the Castle Homes office. I want to let them know what happened and see if we can discover who was driving that truck."

Dave was talking to another couple when they stepped into the office. A young female receptionist approached them and asked if she could help. Noah explained what had happened and that they needed to learn the name of the driver.

The other couple left the office with brochures and maps in hand and Dave stepped toward them. "Did I overhear that you folks had a problem?"

Noah repeated what he had told the receptionist. "Who was driving the truck? The guy needs to be reprimanded."

"Of course. I'm so sorry for what happened and relieved you weren't hurt."

"Gravel chipped my windshield, and we could have been severely injured."

"I'm sure Castle Homes will cover the damage as soon as we talk to the driver." He pulled out his phone. "I'll call the foreman. He'll locate the driver so we can get to the bottom of this situation."

He tapped in a number and raised the phone to his ear, nodding when the call was answered. He repeated the information.

"You're sure?" He frowned and then sighed. "I'll pass on the information."

Disconnecting, he turned to Ruthie and Noah. "The foreman says we don't have any dump trucks on the worksite today and no orders for gravel deliveries. He wondered if you confused the truck with another possible buyer who was touring the housing sites."

"Buyers don't usually drive dump trucks filled with gravel."

"You're right, sir. The foreman's down by the lake if you want to talk to him. I'm sorry I can't be of more help."

Ruthie and Noah left the office and climbed into the pickup. "I have caused too many problems," she said as she buckled her seat belt.

"You weren't the one driving the dump truck. We'll try to find that truck. The Castle foreman may think he didn't have a gravel delivery today, but we didn't imagine the truck and his aggressive driving."

They scoured the building site without success. "Let's head to the lake," Noah said finally. "I want to talk to the foreman personally."

But the only work crews they saw were carpenters

stubbing a new home. Noah pulled to a stop near one of the workmen.

"I'm looking for the foreman. Have you seen Brian Burkholder?"

The guy shook his head. "Not today."

"Dave, at the office, said we'd find him here," Noah explained.

The workman glanced around the site as if searching for the foreman. "Sorry, sir. He must be working somewhere else."

"We might as well go," Ruthie advised. "We've driven around the entire area."

"Yet Dave talked to the foreman." Noah sighed. "Which only confirms my suspicions about this whole development and Castle Homes in particular. As I said before, something's fishy."

The workman tapped another man's shoulder and pointed to Noah's truck. The guy shook his head and approached.

Bending down, he peered at Noah through the passenger window Ruthie had lowered. "You folks are looking for the foreman?"

Noah nodded. "That's right."

"Drive down that road." The guy indicated a narrow lane on the far side of the lake. "He's got a trailer about half a mile from here. If he's not on-site, you can usually find him there."

"We appreciate your help."

Noah circled the lake and passed a house in the final stages of completion.

Ruthie tugged on his arm and pointed to the mountain. "The valley is even more visible from here."

He nodded. "You're right about shifting the direction of the river, especially at the source. Trying to divert the flow of water farther down the mountain from our properties would be more difficult."

"Castle is promising a lake and Prescott Construction is buying your land, and maybe mine, in hopes of selling Castle the water access he needs for a huge profit."

"Although," Noah said, "Castle could have made us an offer himself instead of going through Prescott Construction."

"*Yah*, but perhaps Burkholder did not tell his boss how he plans to get the water, especially if he hopes to make money from the deal."

"If Burkholder is going behind the boss's back, he might be getting anxious. Maybe he sent the notes and attacked you to ensure you would sell so the deal would go through in a timely manner."

"Yet he has not attacked you," she added.

"Because he's convinced I will sell, Ruthie. You received the offer from Prescott Construction when you stopped at the post office. How long ago had the letter been mailed?"

"Almost six weeks ago. Do you think Brian Burkholder feared I would not sell so he decided to scare me off the property?"

"Crazy as it sounds, I think that was his plan."

She hugged her arms. "We need to call Deputy Warren and tell him to question Burkholder. Then I want to get Simon and Andrew and return home, Noah."

"Let's locate the trailer before I call the deputy. After that we'll make a fast stop for paint so I can work on the chicken coop."

She nodded. "If we must, but I am worried. Not about the mountain property, but about the boys. With everything that has happened, I do not like having them out of my sight."

"Then we'll wait until another day to get the paint and go directly to your aunt's house."

"Ben said I was too protective, but I watched my mother's condition become life-threatening in a short time."

"I remember. Your father blamed you."

She nodded. "He waited too long to go for the midwife. Deep down, he probably knew he had made a mistake, but it was easier to say my inattentiveness had somehow caused her death."

Noah rubbed her hand. "I'm sure the boys are fine."

"I pray they are, but my anxiety will not ease until I see for myself."

"We'll drive just a bit farther before we turn around. I'd like to ensure that guy was telling the truth about the foreman's trailer."

As Noah steered the pickup away from the curb, Ruthie tugged on his arm. "Look at that house."

A team of men were painting the trim. "Notice the man carrying the bucket of paint?"

The guy was tall and muscular. He wore a short-sleeve shirt. His left arm was covered with tattoos.

"That is the man who returned the envelope to me at the library. The man who was living in the woods. He must have gotten a job with the painting company."

"Can you be certain it's the same man?" Noah asked.

"He looks like the same man, but—"

Ruthie flicked her gaze around the construction site searching for the missing gravel truck before she turned back to stare at him. He glanced at her, then nodded as if he recognized her.

Her stomach knotted. After seeing his face, she was sure he was the man at the library. Was he also the man on the mountain? Could he be the man who had driven the gravel truck or the red pickup?

NINETEEN

After leaving the lake area, Noah drove along the dirt road that flanked the back of the cleared housing development. He pointed to a trailer in the distance that was parked in a small thicket of trees.

"Looks like Burkholder found a little shade for his trailer," he said to Ruthie.

"I do not want him to see us, Noah. We need to turn around and head back to town."

At that moment, a red truck sped around the trailer and headed toward them.

Ruthie screamed. Noah turned the wheel and drove off the road. The truck accelerated and raced past them.

A red truck with tinted windows.

"Oh, Noah," Ruthie gasped. "That was the third time today we have almost been in an accident."

"But nothing was accidental about any of those near collisions. Did you see the driver, Ruthie? I'm sure it was Brian Burkholder."

"I only saw a blur as the truck passed. The same truck that shoved us onto the train tracks."

"You're right about that." Noah pulled out his phone and tapped in a number. "I'm calling Deputy Warren."

The call went to voice mail. Noah explained what they had discovered. "We think Brian Burkholder just left the area in a red truck."

He disconnected and pocketed his phone. "Let's take

a closer look before we turn around. Then I'll try to call Deputy Warren again."

He parked beside the trailer. "Wait in the pickup."

She shook her head. "I'm going with you."

Together they hurried to the side door. Noah knocked. When no one answered, he knocked again.

Leaning toward the window, he cupped his hands around his eyes to cut down on the glare and stared inside.

The interior of the trailer looked like a tornado had spun through the confined space. Papers were tossed helter-skelter. A coffee cup had been overturned on a table. Another cup was shattered.

Stretching to see more of the chaos, Noah groaned.

Ruthie tugged on his arm. "What is it?"

"Someone's on the floor. He isn't moving."

Noah rapped on the window. "Brian? Brian Burkholder?"

"Noah, this frightens me."

"Go back to my truck, Ruthie."

She glanced over her shoulder and then shook her head. "I am not going anywhere without you."

He pulled out a handkerchief, wrapped it around the doorknob and opened the door.

A cloying, acrid smell of blood wafted past him. "Stay outside, Ruthie."

He stepped into the confusion. "Brian?"

The man pictured in the Castle Homes poster—the same man they had seen at the pizza parlor—was lying in the middle of the trailer. His mouth gaped open.

Kneeling, Noah felt for a pulse. When he withdrew his hand, it was covered with blood.

Peering from the doorway, Ruthie gasped.

"Don't touch anything. I'll call Deputy Warren again."

"What do you think happened?"

"Someone got to him."

"The man driving the red truck?" Ruthie asked.

"I'm not sure." Noah glanced at the shelf behind the table. "Look at that framed photograph of a young man."

He leaned closer. "It says, 'Thanks for being such a great dad! Your son, Prescott.'"

Ruthie's eyes widened. "Brian Burkholder named the construction company after his son."

Noah wiped his hand on his handkerchief, then hit Redial on his phone.

The deputy answered.

Noah repeated the information he had left on voice mail and explained again that they were at Castle Homes and had gone searching for the foreman. He mentioned that the man who had returned Ruthie's letter in the library was painting homes in the area and also told him about the red truck that had raced past them.

"We found the foreman in his trailer," Noah said at last. "But he's dead."

"Can you identify the body, ma'am?" Deputy Warren stared at Ruthie. Noah stepped closer and put his arm around her shoulder.

"Is this the same man who attacked you at your home?" the deputy asked.

She glanced at the dead man and blinked back tears. "I do not know. He has the same build, but as I told you, the man who accosted me wore a stocking over his face."

"What about the tattoos on his arm?" The deputy had lifted his sleeve so she could see the markings.

"I do not know if they are what I saw on the man who attacked me. The colors look different. I cannot be sure."

"The red truck that raced past you looked like the vehicle that pushed you into the way of the oncoming train?"

She nodded. "*Yah*, this is so. We thought Brian Burkholder was driving the truck, but then we discovered his body in the trailer."

The crime-scene investigators were going through the trailer searching for evidence. The coroner had proclaimed Brian Burkholder dead and his body would soon be taken to the morgue so the pathologist could do an autopsy.

The foreman had been stabbed three times in the chest, which appeared to be the cause of death, although the pathologist would make the final determination.

"We've got some of our guys tracking down Vince Ashcroft, the real-estate agent." Deputy Warren glanced at Noah. "If the two of them worked together and if Mr. Burkholder tried to coerce either of you into turning over your property to him without telling his partner, Ashcroft could have gotten angry and decided to take matters into his own hands. We'll talk to Mr. Castle and see what kind of an agreement he had with Prescott Construction."

"Check out Chattanooga," Noah suggested. "I have a hunch Burkholder was involved in that dam collapse."

"Will do." The deputy's phone rang. He pulled it to his ear. "Deputy Warren."

Turning away from Noah and Ruthie, he conversed with the caller, then disconnected, pocketed his phone and stepped back to them. "The red pickup's been found. It belongs to the assistant foreman, John Zimmer. Evidently, he also goes by the name Zimmerman. He's definitely a person of interest. As soon as we can locate him, we'll haul him in for questioning."

"See if he has tattoos on his left arm," Ruthie said.

"Will do, ma'am."

The deputy glanced at the notes he had taken. "I've got everything I need from both of you. Where can I find you if I need any additional information?"

Ruthie looked at Noah. "I feel sure Aunt Mattie would let us stay with her."

He nodded. "That sounds like a good plan, at least until the deputy assures us the murderer is behind bars."

Ruthie provided her aunt's address.

Deputy Warren wrote the address on his tablet. "I'll have one of our guys follow you to your aunt's farm. Use caution until we make an arrest."

He turned to Noah. "How's cell coverage at the aunt's house?"

"Hopefully better than on the mountain. You've got my number?"

The deputy nodded. "I'll let you know as soon as we find the killer."

Noah shook the deputy's hand. "Thanks for your help."

Ruthie felt even more unsettled as they left the crime scene. A man had died, and another man was being hunted down. Was he the man who had come after her?

There were so many people of interest, as the deputy had mentioned. One of them wanted to do Ruthie and her children harm. Seeing how the killer had stabbed Brian Burkholder only compounded her worry. She had known the man who had attacked her was vile, but he had grown more brazen and his attacks more threatening. Now, without a shadow of a doubt, he not only wanted to do her harm, he also wanted to kill her.

Thinking of the danger she and her children were in made her tremble.

She glanced back and let out a sigh of relief when she saw the sheriff's deputy following them.

"How soon will it be over, Noah?" she asked.

"Hopefully before long, Ruthie, although we need to be careful until the perpetrator is apprehended."

"Poor Tiffany. She could be working for a killer."

"I regret taking you to his real-estate office. And to think we considered having him sell our land."

"The *Englisch* have strange ideas about the Amish. Some think we are ignorant of our rights and legal standing. He probably thought my farm would go into foreclosure if he forced me to leave."

Noah nodded. "Then he could buy your property at a cut-rate price."

"If not for you, Noah, I might have left permanently for fear of what he would do to Simon and Andrew."

Noah reached out and squeezed her hand. "I'm glad I could help."

"My mother always quoted the Scripture that says, 'With *Gott*, all things work together for good.'"

"Your mother was a wise woman. *Gott* prompted me to return to the mountain and take care of my father's property."

"At the perfect time." Ruthie glanced again at the sheriff's car behind them. Perhaps the worst had passed, especially if they could stay at Aunt Mattie's farm where Ashcroft or Zimmer or whoever killed the foreman and had attacked her would not find them. The killer would be arrested, she was certain, and all her fears would be put to rest.

"I'm eager to see the boys," she told Noah. "It seems like more than a few hours since we left them. So much has happened."

"Reconnecting with your aunt Mattie was a good thing, Ruthie."

"*Yah*, I see *Gott's* hand in this as if He is inviting me back to the Amish community."

"You would receive help and support."

"The boys would enjoy having friends and returning

to the Amish school. I have tried to teach them, but they miss seeing other children."

"All that will change now."

Noah's words reassured her. The killer needed to be apprehended first, then she and her sons could return home.

Would Noah return to his father's home, as well? He had wanted to sell the farm, but the Prescott Construction deal was a thing of the past.

Perhaps now he would decide to stay and rejoin the Amish faith. The thought of having Noah as a neighbor warmed her heart for a moment until everything that had happened came back into focus. Once her attacker was arrested, she could relax. Until then, she needed to be cautious and careful. The vile man had come after her before. As long as he was free to roam the mountain, he would come after her again.

TWENTY

Ruthie knew Noah was as upset as she was about finding the foreman murdered. A light rain shower fell as they left town and drove to Mattie's house. At the turnoff, Noah raised his hand in farewell to the sheriff's deputy who had followed them along the country road. The deputy honked, turned around in the drive and headed back to town.

Andrew was on the covered porch cranking the ice-cream churn when Noah parked in front of the quaint Amish farmhouse. Mattie rose from the porch rocking chair and hurried down the steps to greet them, ignoring the rain.

"Where's Simon?" Ruthie asked, a note of concern in her voice as she took her aunt's outstretched hand.

"Resting inside."

The two women dashed up the steps to the porch.

"His stomach hurts, and he looks pale," Mattie explained. "I am glad you returned early. When he was not interested in churning ice cream, I knew something was wrong."

Ruthie hugged Andrew and placed the palm of her hand on his forehead, relieved that he felt cool.

"Do you want ice cream, *Mamm*?" he asked. "It is almost ready."

"You are working hard, Andrew. Let me check on Simon first."

"He is sick."

Which is what Ruthie feared. She hurried inside and found Simon resting in the downstairs guest room. One glance at his flushed face and glassy eyes and she knew his upset stomach was caused by more than eating too much cake.

"What hurts?" she asked, running her hand over his hot cheeks.

"Everything."

"Are you nauseous?"

He nodded. "And my head is pounding."

She turned a worried gaze to Noah, who had followed her inside along with Mattie.

His expression confirmed he was equally concerned about Simon's condition. "Do you have a doctor who sees the boys in town?"

"Simon and Andrew are rarely sick, and I have not had the need." She looked again at her son's feverish gaze and weary eyes. "Until now."

"Doctors are always on duty at the emergency room." Mattie stepped closer. "Take Simon to the hospital in town. I have money in the bank in case you are worried about the cost. Andrew can stay here with me. We will eat ice cream, and he can help me bake cookies. I will fix enough dinner for all of you to enjoy, and you can spend the night if it is late when you return from town."

"I had hoped we could stay with you until a bad man is apprehended." Ruthie explained some of what had happened, taking care not to say too much in front of Simon.

"You, Noah and the boys are always welcome here. My house is larger than I need. Having it filled with family will bring me joy."

"Thank you, Mattie." Ruthie hugged her aunt. "You are too kind to give us lodging. Knowing Andrew is with you when we take Simon to the hospital will calm my worry as well, at least for my one son. Plus, if Andrew stays with you, he will not be exposed to other people's germs."

She turned to Noah and grabbed his hand. "I have not asked if you mind driving us back to town."

"Mind? Of course not. Simon needs to see a doctor."

Working together, they eased Simon to his feet and slowly walked him outside. The rain had stopped, but the air was thick with humidity.

"I do not feel good," the boy moaned as Noah helped him into the truck. Ruthie slid in, wrapped her arm around him and positioned Simon's head on her shoulder. Heat radiated from his body, and she feared his temperature had risen even higher than when she first touched his forehead.

Noah climbed behind the wheel. The worry in his expression mirrored her own inner turmoil.

Ruthie had been so focused on the man who had come after them, and then on the idea of selling the land, that she had been less than attentive to Simon this morning. Could he have had the fever earlier without her realizing he was sick?

"Did you think Simon seemed ill this morning?" she asked Noah, hoping for confirmation that she had not neglected her son's care.

"He and Andrew were in great spirits when we drove down the hill," Noah replied. "The illness has come on quickly."

His response eased her concern that she had ignored some sign of his ill health this morning. "Simon never gets sick."

"The weather has been bad, especially with all the rain. I shouldn't have let the boys help me fix the bridge."

"That did not make him sick. This is something else, but I do not know what it could be."

"The doctor will be able to diagnose the problem."

Ruthie closed her eyes. Gott, *please let it be so.*

* * *

The emergency room was filled with sick people. Many were coughing and holding their heads. Some were wrapped in blankets, or leaned against loved ones for support.

Noah found three chairs in the corner. He and Simon remained there while Ruthie headed to the end of a long line of people waiting at the registration desk. After slowly making her way to the front, she accepted a stack of forms from the clerk and returned to where Noah and Simon sat to fill them out.

Simon started to shiver. Noah asked for a blanket and then held the forms while Ruthie tucked the covering around her son.

Glancing down at the top paper, Noah's gaze homed in on the block for father's name. Ruthie had written Benjamin Eicher.

A heavy weight settled over Noah's shoulders. Even though he hadn't known about Ruthie's pregnancy, Noah had given up his right to be called Simon's father when he left the mountain ten years ago. No matter how much it pained him now, he had to realize the truth. He was not part of Ruthie's family, no matter how much he wanted to be.

Simon's face was pale, and he continued to shiver even with the blanket. Ruthie pulled him closer and rubbed her hand over his forehead. Her face was tight with worry.

Noah patted her hand, hoping to offer support. She smiled weakly as if grateful for his presence.

"As I mentioned earlier, I have never had to use the emergency room before." She glanced at the crowd of sick patients waiting to be seen. "This is not how I expected it to be."

It was still daylight. Knowing how illness often struck

in the middle of the night, Noah feared the crowded conditions could get much worse.

Within the hour, Simon was called into a triage room. The nurse listened to Ruthie's explanation of his symptoms before she took his vitals.

"His temperature is one hundred and three degrees," the nurse announced. "Blood pressure is normal, pulse is elevated. His oxygen level is ninety-eight."

"What does that mean?" Ruthie asked.

"It means he'll have to wait to see a doctor."

She handed Simon a pill and a glass of water. "This should bring down his fever. After he takes the medication, return to the waiting room and we'll call you shortly."

Shortly turned into two hours.

The nurse took Simon's temperature again. "It's one hundred two point eight degrees. The doctor will be in soon."

The physician was an older gentleman with tired eyes and a sagging jaw. He examined Simon, then ordered blood work and rapid flu and strep tests.

"I'll be back with the lab results," he assured them as he left the room.

Simon fell asleep on the cot, and Ruthie and Noah sat nearby as they waited even longer for the results to come back from the lab.

"He's a good son," Ruthie whispered to Noah.

"You've done a great job raising him."

"He brings me so much joy. He looked like you even as a baby. Sometimes I marveled that people did not realize who his father really was."

"I'm sorry, Ruthie. I had no idea."

"We cannot undo the past."

The doctor returned with the lab results. "The cultures will take another twenty-four to forty-eight hours before we can identify the organism, but I can tell you for certain that your son has a serious infection. Do you have a well, Mrs. Eicher?"

"*Yah*, we do."

"Has the well water been tested recently?"

"I do not know that it has ever been checked."

"With all this rain, we're seeing an increase in contamination. Pasture runoff often causes problems. Get your water checked. I'll notify Public Health and ask them to send someone to your house."

"No one is there now."

"Not to worry—it'll take them a few days to get to you. Until then, I'd buy a kit at the hardware store so you can check for various contaminants. One will be for bacteria. It won't differentiate which organisms are causing problems, but it will let you know if bacteria has gotten into your water supply. Until you talk to the Public Health folks, boil your water for at least a minute, then cool it in a sealed container before you use it."

"I have heard people mention having to shock their wells. Is this something I must do if I find contamination?" she asked.

"Public Health can help you with that. They'll provide guidelines on how much bleach to use." He made a note on a clipboard. "Let's keep Simon overnight so we can get his temperature down. I want to ensure he doesn't develop complications."

More time passed until they got a room and then admitted Simon. Once he was settled in his hospital bed, Ruthie put her head in her hands.

Noah rubbed her shoulder. "He's going to be okay."

"If what the doctor said is true, I allowed the boys to drink tainted water."

"Wait until the well is tested before you jump to conclusions, and remember that contamination happens. Most folks test their water twice a year."

She bit her lip. "Which proves that Simon's illness is my fault for not ensuring the water was safe."

"You heard the doctor. The increased rainfall could be the reason."

"What if the man tampered with the well? So much has happened. He told me he would hurt my children."

She shook her head and glanced away, as if not wanting Noah to see her upset.

"Right now, focus on Simon getting better," he encouraged. "I'll go to the cafeteria and bring back some food. You haven't eaten since breakfast."

"Food would be *gut*, and some water. Clean water that will not cause infection." She wrung her hands. "If the water is bad, then Andrew could get sick, as well."

"He was fine when we left him."

"*Yah*, and I pray he continues to be all right." She hesitated a moment and then added, "Two milk bottles were in a bucket of cool water overnight. Simon drank milk from an open bottle that was almost empty. Andrew's milk was poured from the new bottle. Suppose the man tampered with the open bottle of milk?"

"The lab tests will determine what caused Simon's illness. Tomorrow we can check on Andrew. Until then, we will stay with Simon and pray his condition improves."

Ruthie would pray for Simon's condition to improve and for Andrew to remain healthy. She would also pray for law enforcement to capture Brian Burkholder's killer and the man who wanted to do her and her boys harm.

How much longer would they have to live life looking over their shoulders? She wanted everything resolved as fast as possible. Bottom line, she wanted her family to be healthy and safe.

TWENTY-ONE

Noah hurried to the cafeteria and returned with hamburgers and fries. Ruthie hardly touched the food, but she drank the bottle of water.

After he had eaten, Noah settled into an easy chair in the corner of the room. Ruthie rested in a recliner next to Simon's bed. She closed her eyes and was soon asleep.

Simon's breathing was even, but his coloring remained pale. Before coming back to the mountain, Noah hadn't known he had a son. Now he worried he might lose the boy he had grown to love in just a short time. Truth be told, he had loved him that first night when he had seen him in the light of the oil lamp. The similarity between them was so great there had been no question that Simon was his son.

If Noah had known Ruthie was pregnant ten years ago, he never would have left her. His father couldn't mail Ruthie's letter because Noah hadn't told him where he and Seth were living. He had communicated with his father much later, but by that time, Ruthie's letters would have been long forgotten.

Noah drew closer to the bed and touched his son's cheek. "*Gott*, it has been a long time since I have talked to You. I've made a lot of mistakes. Not being here for my son is one of them. Get him through this illness, then help Ruthie find a good man to help her with the boys. She deserves a better life than she's had. Provide for her needs. I'll set up a fund for Simon and Andrew. Both boys are so special. If Seth hadn't died, I might be ready to open my heart again, but I seem to make a mess of everything You've given me that is good. Don't let me hurt Ruthie or Simon again. Please."

Noah stood at the side of the bed for a long time while Simon and Ruthie slept. Throughout the night he continued to pray for his son, and for Ruthie and Andrew, and asked the Lord to bring good from all the pain.

Ruthie woke with a start when the nurse entered the room early the next morning. She sat up, rubbed her eyes and glanced around, unable to find Noah.

"I'm sorry to disturb you," the nurse said with an apologetic smile. "Your husband went to get coffee and something to eat. He said to tell you he'd be back in a flash if you awoke."

"My husband?"

The nurse nodded. "Yes, ma'am. He's been awake all night and stopped by the nurses' desk a number of times asking about his son. We tried to reassure him, but he has been quite anxious."

Ruthie nodded. "We both have been concerned."

"Everything appears worse in the middle of the night." The nurse studied the monitor. "Simon's vitals look good. I'll get his temp in a minute. The phlebotomist will be in soon to draw his blood."

"More tests?"

"I'm afraid so. The doctor wants to ensure he's improving."

Ruthie stood and neared the bed. "Looks like he is a sleepyhead this morning."

"It's early. I'll come back in a bit for that temp. I hate to bother patients, especially when they're sleeping so soundly." She hung another antibiotic bag and left the room.

Ruthie raked her fingers through her hair and repositioned her *kapp*. She stepped into the bathroom, then splashed water on her face and rinsed her mouth.

After returning to Simon's bedside, she glanced out the window. A low cloud cover fell over the countryside. From the dark sky, more rain seemed likely. She was concerned about the rising water.

Once before, the river had flooded. Her mother had been alive, and they had moved the few furnishings they had upstairs. She had had the foresight to take bread and jam and some nonperishable food items to the second floor, along with jugs of water.

"*Gott* will provide" had been her mother's response as the water rose.

Ruthie had been little and remembered looking across the rain-swollen river to Noah's house. His home sat higher on the mountain and escaped the flood.

For two days, Ruthie and her family had holed up in the hot upstairs, and then the rain had stopped and the sun appeared.

"*Gott* has answered our prayers," her mother had said with her usual optimism.

Within twelve hours the water had left the house, although mud and debris remained on the first floor and had to be swept out and mopped clean. Noah and his family came to help, and by the second day, the floorboards were damp but free from the mud. *Mamm* had aired out the house for days. The sun and a mountain breeze had been in their favor.

At that time, *Datt* had been a jovial man with a ready smile and hugs for his daughter. He had changed after her mother had died.

"Breakfast."

She turned at the sound of Noah's voice and smiled.

His hair was somewhat disheveled and his eyes were tired, but he was as handsome as the young man who had stolen her heart years ago.

"Two coffees, plus platters of eggs and sausage. Also croissants and fresh fruit."

"Croissants?"

"Something different, *yah*?"

She nodded. "*Yah*. But the food smells delicious and I am hungry."

"How's our patient?"

"Sleeping soundly, which is probably good. The nurse did not want to wake him to take his temperature. She will return in a bit."

"So we can enjoy our meal without interruption from the medical staff."

"The phlebotomist is due shortly."

"What did the nurse say about Simon?"

"The results of the lab tests will provide more information."

Ruthie bowed her head. Noah was silent until she glanced up.

"Enjoy the food," he said.

"You always anticipate my needs, Noah."

"I was awake and hungry. I knew you would want to eat, as well. Don't give me more credit than I deserve."

"You deserve a lot of credit."

"I deserve a lot of blame, as well. I should have stayed, Ruthie."

"You needed to make your own way."

"At your expense. A good man would not leave someone he loved behind."

Her heart pounded with Noah's words. He had loved her. If only circumstances had been different.

A knock sounded at the door. "Morning. I'm Janice, from the lab."

"Simon is still sleeping."

"I've got a few more patients to draw on this floor. How 'bout I come back in a few minutes? You can enjoy your breakfast a little longer."

"That is very thoughtful. Thank you."

Ruthie ate in silence, unwilling to meet Noah's gaze. She needed to keep her focus on the present and take each moment as it came.

Noah is leaving, her voice of reason continued to warn her.

Plus, he was *Englisch*.

She steeled her spine and reached for the coffee. She would not let her heart be broken again. Once was one time too many. If it happened a second time, she might not survive.

TWENTY-TWO

Noah was anxious to hear what the doctor had to say, but it was late morning before the physician made his rounds.

"How are you feeling?" the doctor asked after he had poked and prodded Simon's stomach, listened to his heart, and checked his pupils.

"I am hungry," the boy announced. His face was pale and he still had a fever.

The doctor glanced at the breakfast tray. "You didn't eat breakfast."

"I would like real food like my *mamm* cooks," Simon explained, "instead of watery cream of wheat and dry toast."

The doctor nodded. "I'll have dietary change you to a nonrestrictive diet. Lunch should be more appetizing."

"Gut," Simon said with a weak smile.

"How does your head feel?"

"Like it is stuffed with cotton. My stomach is better, but it rumbles."

"You were a sick young man when you came in." The doctor glanced at Simon's file. "Your condition has improved, but only slightly, which concerns me. We need to be sure the antibiotic is working."

"When can he go home?" Ruthie asked.

"Not this soon. We'll see how he does tonight. Tomorrow might be a different story."

After the doctor left, Simon turned to his mother. "Why do I have to stay here?"

"Because you are sick."

"What about Andrew?"

"He is at Aunt Mattie's house, though I am concerned he might be sick, as well."

"I could check on him," Noah suggested.

"I would rather see for myself that he is all right."

Noah's phone rang. He stepped into the hallway and nodded when he heard Deputy Warren's voice.

"I wanted to give you an update," the deputy said. "We questioned Vince Ashcroft, the real-estate agent. He was in on the land-acquisition deal with Burkholder and Zimmer. Evidently the assistant foreman had come up with the initial concept of redirecting the mountain water, but Burkholder claimed it was his own idea when he talked to Mr. Castle. Zimmer became belligerent and the two argued."

"So you think Zimmer killed the foreman?"

"He's more than a person of interest at this point. Our guys went over his red truck from top to bottom. Guess what they found under the driver's seat?"

"A knife."

"You got that right. No prints but he probably wiped it clean. There was blood on the blade and we're having Forensics check to see if it matches the foreman's blood."

"As you might recall, a black sedan tried to run into Ruthie and her children when we were in town. Does Zimmer own a second vehicle?"

"No, but the guys at the construction site usually leave their keys in their cars. Easy enough to borrow someone else's set of wheels."

"And what about tattoos?"

"Tell Mrs. Eicher that John Zimmer has tattoos on both arms."

"I'll tell her. Is he in custody?"

"We've spotted him outside of town. I'll let you know when we make the arrest."

After disconnecting, Noah stepped back into the hospital room. Simon was asleep, and Noah kept his voice lowered as he shared the information with Ruthie.

"Are you saying the assistant foreman decided to use force to get me off my land so he could buy the property without going through Prescott Construction?" Ruthie rubbed her hands together.

Noah nodded. "That seems to be right. Evidently he didn't trust Brian Burkholder."

"Greed is an ugly vice," she said.

"And it caused one man to lose his life. Law enforcement is closing in on Zimmer. They've spotted him outside of town."

"I will be glad when he is apprehended."

Noah glanced at the clock on the wall. "Ivan Keim should have checked the buggy by now. I'll walk to the repair shop and drive the buggy back here to the hospital. That way, as soon as Deputy Warren informs us that Zimmer is in custody, you can take the rig to Mattie's house to check on Andrew while I stay with Simon."

Ruthie smiled with relief. "That would be perfect, Noah."

Ruthie hated to see Noah leave the hospital. She had appreciated his support and had been touched by his concern for her son. Their son, she corrected herself.

Simon's eyes fluttered open when the nurse came in to check on his IV bag. "Your husband went home?" she asked Ruthie.

"He is running an errand in town."

"Simon takes after his dad."

The boy glared at Ruthie and nodded his head toward the nurse when her back was turned, as if to say she was totally confused.

"You should have corrected her, *Mamm*," Simon said once the nurse had left the room.

Ruthie shrugged, trying to act nonchalant about the woman's comment. "There is no reason to correct her, Simon. She thinks what she thinks."

"Still, she should be told that Noah is not my *datt*."

"Yet, he is a *gut* man."

"*Yah*, I would be happy to be his son, but it is not so."

Ruthie's stomach was in turmoil. How long would it take before Simon realized the truth?

Knowing he might ask more questions, she remained on edge until he eventually fell asleep.

Her back and hips ached after sitting so long. Needing to stretch her legs, she rose quietly, headed into the hall and then walked at a fast clip to the far end of the hospital wing. Turning, she headed down another hallway and then another, enjoying the chance to get at least a little exercise. Before long she found herself in an older section of the hospital that appeared to be in a remodeling phase.

Realizing she had walked too far, she turned and started to retrace her steps. A noise sounded behind her. She glanced over her shoulder but saw no one. Concerned that she was alone in a secluded area, Ruthie hurried along the hallway and glanced at the overhead signage, needing to determine the way that led back to Simon's wing.

Footsteps sounded behind her. Her heart rate, already elevated from the brisk walk, increased even more.

"Still trying to get away from me?" A man's voice, coarse and belligerent, echoed in the empty hallway.

Glancing over her shoulder, she gasped, seeing his contorted face wedged within a woman's stocking.

"You tried to run from me, Ruthie. Now that I found you, I won't let you get away from me again."

He tried to grab her arm. She saw scratch marks on his hands.

"No!" She shoved past him and ran down the corridor.

He chased after her. His footfalls caused her heart to beat nearly out of her chest.

She was lost in a maze of hospital hallways that all looked alike. As she ran, she tried to read the direction signs.

He was close behind her. Too close.

Her feet slipped on the waxed floor. She screamed, caught herself and raced on again.

Where was the door that led into the main section of the hospital? She had to get away from him and make sure Simon was all right.

Security! She needed hospital security.

"Help!" she cried.

He chuckled—it was a menacing sound that made her pulse race even faster. Fear jammed her throat and twisted along her spine.

Her stomach tightened.

The door dividing the old section of the hospital from the new appeared ahead. She ran full steam against the swinging doors and nearly knocked over an elderly gentleman when she burst into the newer wing.

"Watch where you're going," the man growled.

"I am sorry, sir."

She skirted him and kept running.

Simon.

Everything inside her was screaming for her son. Was he okay or had the hateful man attacked Simon before he had come after her?

Ruthie moaned, unwilling to think about what could have happened.

She turned into Simon's hallway and stopped short outside his room. Pulling in a quick breath, she pushed on the door and stepped into his room, still struggling to regulate her breathing.

Simon's eyes widened. "*Mamm*, what is wrong?"

"Nothing is wrong." She patted her chest in hopes of calming her pulse and her racing heartbeat. "How are you feeling?"

Ruthie glanced over her shoulder. Where was the hateful man? Had he left her, or was he outside the room waiting for her even now?

"You look like you have been running, *Mamm*."

She rubbed her fingers over her son's flushed cheek. "A fast walk for exercise."

"You never could tell a lie."

"What do you mean?"

"I mean you were running. Was someone coming after you?" He glanced at the door, worried.

"You are making more of this than you should. I hurried when I realized how long I had been gone. Did you sleep the whole time?"

"I woke up once and saw a man standing next to my bed."

Fear gripped her heart. "What happened then?"

"He turned around and left the room, and I fell back to sleep. The next time I woke up, he was gone."

Ruthie trembled and her stomach roiled. Was it the same man who had chased after her?

Would he ever leave her and her boys alone?

TWENTY-THREE

Ivan Keim greeted Noah with a warm smile as he entered the buggy shop.

"Your buggy is ready." The shop owner wiped his hands on a towel. "You did a *gut* job reattaching the wheel to the axle. You have worked on buggies before this?"

"My father's buggy had problems over the years. I was his mechanic, but not by choice."

"It is a way to learn. If you need a job, I could use help."

Noah appreciated the offer. "I'm here to sell my father's land, then I'll be moving on."

"This area is a *gut* place to settle down, marry and raise a family."

"I grew up here and am well aware of the benefits."

"You were Amish, *yah*?"

"I was. Perhaps you knew my *datt*. Reuben Schlabach?"

Ivan rubbed his jaw. "Reuben lived on the mountain."

"You knew him?"

"I knew your mother. She was a wonderful woman. Your father was not the same after she died."

"By chance, do you know of Prescott Construction? They are interested in buying my father's land?"

Ivan shrugged. "So much building. We will lose our peace, *yah*, when so many move into the new homes north of town."

"Castle Homes?"

The buggy maker nodded. "He buys farms from the Amish and then destroys the land. It is a shame."

"You've heard he plans to have a lake there."

Pursing his lips, Ivan shook his head. "I do not think his lake will find water."

Noah agreed. He paid Ivan and hitched the mare to the buggy. Leaving the shop, Noah checked the surrounding area. At the next intersection, he spied a tall man in dark clothing hurrying along the sidewalk. If only Ruthie had been able to positively identify the man who had attacked her.

On a hunch, he stopped by the sheriff's office. Deputy Warren was there. "Have you apprehended Zimmer?"

"Not yet, but we're closing in on him."

Noah told him about the man he had seen on the street.

"We'll check it out," Warren said. "And I'll let you know when we have Zimmer in custody."

Noah left, discouraged that the assistant foreman was still at large as he headed back to the hospital. Exiting the elevator on Simon's floor, his heart lurched when he saw hospital security outside the boy's room. He hurried forward to determine the problem.

Ruthie's face was flushed and her eyes wide as she rushed to meet him in the hallway. Quickly, she explained what had happened.

"Did anyone call the sheriff's office?" he asked.

The hospital-security folks shook their heads.

The man who seemed to be in charge stepped closer. "Our guards are searching for the man throughout the hospital, sir, but I haven't notified the sheriff yet."

Noah pulled out his phone. "I'll call his office. I stopped in a few minutes ago and talked to the deputy we saw yesterday, Ruthie. He needs to know Zimmer might be in the area."

"I saw scratches on his arms today," Ruthie said. "I fought back both times he attacked me on the mountain.

I am not sure if I scratched him or if they are from some-one else."

"Scratches on both hands?" he asked.

She nodded. "*Yah*, both hands."

"I'll pass that information on to Deputy Warren."

Noah hit the prompt and connected with the sheriff's department. The deputy came on the line and Noah shared what Ruthie had said about the scratches.

"Security is searching the hospital," Noah explained. "Timing would have been right for the guy who attacked Ruthie to have been the man I saw on the street."

"One of our deputies spotted someone who matches your description in the downtown area. We're closing in."

Noah and Ruthie left hospital security in the hallway and returned to Simon's room. His eyes were closed and he moaned in his sleep.

"How is he?" Noah asked, stepping to the boy's bedside.

"I am not sure. They thought he was improving, then he had a setback."

"Another fever?"

She nodded. "The nurse took his temperature be-fore calling security about the man who came after me. The doctor is concerned Simon's medication might not be working. He said the organism could be resistant. If Simon doesn't show more signs of improvement soon—"

The worry on her face told Noah what he needed to know.

Simon moaned again, then his eyes blinked open.

Noah stepped closer to the bed. "Hey, champ. How are you feeling?"

"*Gut.*" Simon smiled weakly.

Noah squeezed his hand. "Your mom and I are right here with you. You're going to be okay. Get some rest now so the medicine can do its job."

Simon nodded, then closed his eyes and drifted back to sleep.

Ruthie moved to the bedside. "I have never seen him so sick."

"The medicine will work, Ruthie."

"Was it the well water? If so, I fear Andrew could be sick as well, yet I do not want to leave Simon when his fever is still high."

"Do you know anyone who lives near Mattie who has a phone?" Noah asked.

She shook her head. "You are also worried."

"I'm more worried about the man who wants to do you harm."

Ruthie's face was pale. "Too much is happening, Noah. You and I made mistakes in our youth, but I know God provides his mercy. Scripture says, *For where two or three are gathered together in my name, there am I in the midst of them.* We are Simon's parents. My mother always prayed for me and said *Gott* listens when parents pray for their children."

She held out her hand. "Let us put aside our differences and the pain from the past and pray together for the health of this son of ours."

Noah had been the one to make the mistake of leaving Ruthie. She had always done what was right. She loved her son. Noah did, too.

He took her hand and closed his eyes.

Please, Lord, he prayed silently. *Help Simon. Help our son.*

Ruthie's voice faltered as she started to pray aloud. "*Gott*, You know we love Simon. He is a wonderful boy with a huge heart. Noah and I have made mistakes, but we love this child, and we ask for his healing. We also ask that Andrew does not get sick. Stop the man who wants to do us harm and let us both know what to do about our land."

Her eyes fluttered open and Noah's heart nearly burst with love for her.

He stepped closer. "Ruthie, I—"

"Oh, Noah." She stepped into his embrace. All he could think of was her sweetness and how he had always loved her.

He pulled her closer and lowered his lips—

His phone rang.

She stepped away. Confusion lined her face.

"I'm sorry." He raised the phone. "Noah Schlabach."

"We got him." The deputy's voice sounded in Noah's ear. "We've apprehended the guy in black. He's got scratches on his hands. Said he was playing with a stray cat. He's coming in for questioning. I'm hoping we'll get a confession. Stop by my office later and I'll fill you in on more details."

"Thanks. I will."

Noah disconnected and turned back to Ruthie. "They're hauling someone into the sheriff's office. Deputy Warren will interrogate him. They're hoping for a confession."

A tap sounded at the door and the nurse hurried into the room. "Sorry to bother you folks. The doctor wants Simon's temperature checked again."

She nudged the boy. He blinked his eyes open before she placed the thermometer in his mouth. Once the device buzzed, the nurse smiled at Ruthie. "His temp is down a bit, which is encouraging."

"*Gott* is good," Ruthie said. Tears filled her eyes and she took Simon's hand and smiled.

A lunch tray arrived, and Simon sat up and ate slowly. Relief washed over Ruthie's face and joy returned to her gaze.

"The buggy's outside," Noah informed her. "Why don't you ride to Mattie's house and check on Andrew. You'll feel better once you know he's okay."

"You are right, Noah."

"While you're gone, I'll call Willkommen Realty about listing my property with them."

She frowned. "You still plan to sell your land?"

"I do. What about you, Ruthie? Have you decided about your land?"

"My family is buried on the mountain, Noah. My mother and father and baby sister."

And Ruthie's husband, whom she didn't mention. Noah had made a mistake so long ago to leave Ruthie. Another man had taken his place.

Ruthie kissed Simon's cheek. "I will be back as soon as I check on your brother."

"*Mamm*, I want to go home."

"*Yah*, you and I will go home soon."

The boy looked at Noah. "What about you?" he asked. "Will you go home with us, Noah?"

Noah's heart broke seeing Simon's confusion.

"I'll take you and your mother home."

"And then what, Noah?" Ruthie asked.

She looked at him like she had the night he had left her ten years ago.

Noah had made so many mistakes, starting with abandoning Ruthie. He had also lost his brother and his brother's family and didn't deserve to find love or to have a family. No matter how deeply he cared for Ruthie, he could not stay on Amish Mountain. She needed to go on with her life. A life without him.

Ruthie squeezed Simon's hand, then left the room, without saying anything more to Noah.

He didn't blame her. He had left her once. He would leave her again, but she would be better off without him. He knew that to be true, even though his heart would break this time just as it had done before.

TWENTY-FOUR

Tears burned Ruthie's eyes as she left the hospital and hurried to where Noah had hitched the buggy. She rubbed Buttercup's mane. "How are you, girl? Ready to take me to Aunt Mattie's house so we can check on Andrew?"

The horse nuzzled Ruthie's hand as if expecting a treat. "Perhaps Aunt Mattie will have a carrot or an apple for you."

She climbed into the buggy, upset with herself, and flicked the reins. All along she had been concerned about growing attached to Noah. Although she had tried with all her might to keep up her guard, once again she had been pulled in by his charm. Her heart did not have a chance.

Noah had done chores and fixed meals and made her boys take pride in who they were and the jobs they did around the farm. He had taught them to fix fences and how to shore up the barn, and they had helped to check the bridge to ensure it was stable.

Plus, he had given them positive affirmation, and showered them with attention. Both boys had yearned for signs of love from Ben, but he was never one to show his feelings. Ruthie was sure her husband had loved Andrew. She feared he had always harbored resentment toward Simon. Not that she had kept anything from Ben before they were married. She had told him about Noah and their youthful mistake. But Simon was not a mistake.

He had been wanted and loved from the moment she realized she was in the family way.

Before their marriage Ben had been accepting. After the ceremony his true feelings had surfaced.

She wiped the tears from her eyes. Ben was gone. Now she had to take care of her sons. *Please,* Gott, *let Simon continue to get better and keep Andrew from getting sick.*

Before she and the boys returned to the mountain, she needed to get a kit to test her well water. How terrible if contamination had caused Simon's infection.

Dark clouds rolled overhead and the musky scent of rain hung in the air. The wind picked up, and she tightened her grip on the reins. She should have been more aware of the dark clouds in the distance before she started on her journey. Hopefully, she would not be stuck at Mattie's house when she needed to return to the hospital to ensure Simon was improving.

If Andrew was sick, she would take him with her and have him checked by a doctor, as well.

Noah would be there, but soon after that he would sign papers to sell his land through the other real-estate firm in town.

How would she explain his leaving to her boys? They were still struggling with Ben's passing and her father's death, and had all too readily accepted Noah into their lives. Now he would be gone.

"Life is not fair," Ruthie said to herself. She heard disappointment in her own voice, tempered with a bit of anger.

After Ben's death, she had hoped life would get easier, but that was not the case. New problems had arisen one after another, starting with the man who had come after her.

Raindrops fell, gentle ones at first, then bigger drops

that slapped against her skin and dampened her dress and bonnet.

She pulled the blanket around her legs to keep them dry and narrowed her gaze to better see into the distance.

A car raced by and threw water against the buggy.

"Ach!" she groaned, wiping her face and hands on the blanket.

She glanced back, no longer able to see the town in the heavy downpour, and then turned onto the side road that led to Mattie's farm.

The sky grew even darker, and the temperature dropped. Ruthie shivered and stared into the pouring rain to keep the mare on the road and headed in the right direction.

The roar of an automobile sounded behind her. She glanced back and spotted headlights. The car was traveling much too fast. She pulled the mare to the side of the road and waited for it to pass, expecting the vehicle's wheels to splash water that would drench her and the inside of the buggy.

Instead of zooming around her buggy, the auto braked to a stop. Ruthie's heart lurched. She glanced back but was unable to see the driver through the car's tinted windshield. A dark sedan, like the car that had driven onto the curb and almost struck her children.

She flicked the reins. The mare started to trot.

The car accelerated.

Ruthie flicked the reins again. Buttercup increased her speed.

The car swerved around the buggy and braked to a stop.

She drew back on the reins. The mare stopped short and balked.

"Easy, girl."

Ruthie's chest constricted. The driver's door opened and a man stepped out. He was tall and muscular and dressed in black with a woman's stocking over his head.

She leaped from the buggy and started to run.

He ran after her.

She raced toward the woods that edged the roadway, then slipped in the rain-drenched soil but continued on.

"No!" she moaned. When she glanced back, her heart jammed her throat. He was right behind her.

She entered the woods, jumped over a fallen log and kept running.

His heavy footfalls sounded behind her.

Her side ached. Branches scratched her arms and snagged at her dress. A root caught her foot. She flailed her arms to keep from falling.

He grabbed her shoulder. She tumbled to the ground.

He kicked her ribs. The air whizzed from her lungs. She tried to crawl away. Her bonnet and *kapp* flew off. He grabbed her bun and yanked on her hair. She screamed in pain.

"Why were you running away from me?" he demanded.

"Who are you and what do you want?"

"I want your land."

"Are you with Prescott Construction?"

"They wanted to buy the land that belongs to me." He jammed a thumb against his chest.

"What?"

His sleeves were raised, exposing a tattoo that covered his skin and scratches around his wrists on both arms.

"I told you to leave," he said. "Your father wanted the farm to stay in the family. He thought you would run off with that boyfriend of yours."

"My father is dead," she said, confused by the man's ramblings.

"He wrote his will ten years ago, thinking you would abandon him. Our parents divided the land between your father and me when all of it should have gone to me. I'm the youngest. That's the Amish way. But they didn't trust me to farm all the land so they gave me a smaller, rocky portion and gave your father the land along the river."

He ripped off the stocking.

She startled, recognizing her father's brother. "Uncle Henry? *Datt* said you two had reconciled."

He laughed. "I begged forgiveness for my transgressions and for leaving the faith. I told your father we needed to be family again and that I would care for the land after you left if anything happened to him."

"I do not understand what you are saying."

"Your father said you were in love with Reuben Schlabach's son. He thought you would leave the farm and the Amish way of life so he had a will drawn up. You were to inherit the farm upon his death, but if you left the property, the land would automatically go to me."

"My *datt* thought I would abandon him?"

"Because you loved the Schlabach boy."

"But I did not leave with Noah."

"Yet the will remains. That's why I wanted you to leave. With you gone, the land would pass to me. I agreed to sell it to Prescott Construction, but today, I learned the foreman planned to double-cross me. He said he could buy the land on his own and didn't need me. Now he's out of the picture."

"You killed Brian Burkholder."

Her uncle sneered. "I made it look like Zimmer, the assistant foreman, killed him."

"I do not believe what you are saying," she countered, hoping her prideful uncle would reveal more information.

"The foreman and assistant foreman had argued recently," he told her.

Ruthie's ploy had worked, as he continued to talk.

"I borrowed Zimmer's red truck to make it seem like he was coming after you," he said.

Ruthie egged him on. "So you planted the murder weapon in his pickup?"

Henry nodded. "My plan worked. Law enforcement arrested him. He'll stand trial and go to jail, while I sell your land directly to Mr. Castle for far more than the foreman planned to give me."

"You do not care about the farm staying in the family. You only care about yourself."

"I gave you an opportunity to leave the mountain, but you were too stubborn. Now you'll have an accident on your farm that will take your life. The river is rising. How tragic if you die in the flood."

"No!"

"Get up. We're going back to my car."

"I am not going anywhere."

"You will unless you want me to harm Andrew."

Her blood froze. "Do not hurt my child."

He jerked on her arm. She stumbled to her feet.

"If you do what I say, the boy won't be harmed."

He tugged her arm behind her back. She gasped. The pain seared along her spine.

"You do not know where to find Andrew," she insisted.

"Don't be a fool. You can't hide anything from me, including your son. I've got him, and you won't be able to find him. Unless you cooperate."

Her heart nearly broke. "I will do whatever you say, but do not hurt Andrew."

He shoved her through the underbrush to where his car was parked and grabbed rope from the backseat. Working quickly, he tied her hands and feet and shoved her into the trunk.

"No, please. I will not cause a problem. Do not leave me in here."

"Just for a short while."

He slammed the trunk closed.

Her heart pounded nearly out of her chest.

She heard the creaking of the buggy. Was he hiding the rig in the wooded area? Few people traveled the road to Mattie's house. If the buggy was out of sight, no one would know she had been captured.

Noah was at the hospital waiting for her return. Mattie was at her house. How long would it be until someone realized she had disappeared?

Heart in her throat, Ruthie felt the engine start and the car begin to move.

If only Noah would come to find her, yet with the buggy out of view, he would never know what happened.

She raised her legs and kicked, trying to force open the trunk, but it held and she remained locked in darkness. Tears burned her eyes and her heart broke thinking she might never see her boys and Noah again.

Simon slept fitfully. Each time he woke, he asked for his *mamm*.

Noah glanced at his watch. Ruthie hadn't been gone long, but he was concerned. Soon after she left, the sky had turned dark and a terrible storm had unleashed its fury.

He should have insisted on driving to Mattie's farm while Ruthie stayed with Simon. Although as upset as she had been about Andrew, she probably wouldn't have agreed.

Noah had thought getting away from the hospital for a short time would be good for her. Now he envisioned her soaking wet and struggling to keep the buggy on the road.

Once she arrived at her aunt's house and found Andrew doing well, he hoped she would remain there until the storm passed.

Noah checked the weather app on his phone. Rain was expected to continue well into the night.

Simon woke again. "Where's *Mamm*?"

"She went to Aunt Mattie's house to check on Andrew. She will return soon."

Simon glanced at the window and saw the downpour. "I worry she will have trouble in this storm."

Noah was worried, too.

Please, Gott, he prayed. *Protect Ruthie and keep her safe.*

TWENTY-FIVE

The car stopped. Ruthie pulled up her legs, ready to strike. When the trunk opened, she kicked her uncle in the chest. He yanked her up and shoved her out of the car. A sharp piece of metal dug into her arm. She gasped and tried to butt him with her head.

"You never give up, do you? But you can't outsmart me."

"Where is Andrew?"

"I won't tell you."

"You are hateful."

He laughed. "You should have cooperated and left the mountain so I wouldn't have to use force."

"Why does Mr. Castle want the land?"

"Your farm and the Schlabach property sit at the source of the river. Redirecting the water at your end will send the river down a northern valley."

"So Castle Homes can have water to fill the lake, but what happens if the river cannot be diverted?"

"I can make it happen once the land is mine, but time is running out. Castle needs the lake filled by next week. I agreed to provide the water. If you hadn't delayed, I would already have the detour completed and the money in my bank account."

"You are hurting the farmers south of town who rely on the river."

"That's not my problem." He untied her legs but kept

hold of her arm and shoved her forward. "Now get going into your house."

Ruthie stared at the churning river that had started to overflow its banks.

She thought back to her youth when the river had flooded and water had come into the house. She feared it would happen again. If only she could overpower the man and escape his grasp.

Where was Andrew? She would do nothing to bring harm to either of her sons. She would rather die herself than have anything happen to her boys.

Noah became increasingly concerned about Ruthie as the storm continued to pummel the area. Lightning cut through the sky and thunder roared.

He took Simon's hand. "How are you feeling?"

"Better. My head and stomach no longer hurt."

"Can you stay alone here at the hospital for a while? I need to drive to Aunt Mattie's house. Your mother went there to check on Andrew. She probably hasn't returned due to the storm. I'll bring her back in my truck."

"I will be fine. Do not worry about me."

"You're a good boy, Simon. Your mother's proud of you and so am I."

He smiled and Noah noticed a brightness in his eyes, which was encouraging.

"I'll come back as soon as I can."

"Be careful, Noah. This storm is bad."

He stopped at the desk to inform the nurse he was leaving.

"I'll keep checking on Simon," she assured him. "I have ice cream that I'm sure he would like for a snack."

Noah thanked the nurse, then hurried outside and ran to his truck. His clothes were drenched by the time he slipped behind the wheel. He shoved the key in the ignition and pulled out of the parking lot as the rain intensified. The day turned dark as night and thunder rumbled overhead.

His cell rang. He hit speed dial and turned the phone to speaker. Deputy Warren's voice.

"We hauled in that guy who lived in the woods and returned Mrs. Eicher's letter the day you visited the library."

"I told you Ruthie and I saw him yesterday at the Castle Home site. He's working for one of the painters."

"And claims he's renting a room and plans to make a better life for himself."

"You don't believe him?" Noah asked.

"I wasn't satisfied with some of Zimmer's responses. He's still being detained, but I'm not certain we've got the right guy."

"You think the man in the woods could be the killer?"

"I'm not sure, that's why I wanted to talk to him. He saw you and Mrs. Eicher heading to the foreman's trailer yesterday. He also saw the red truck racing along the lake road soon after you and Mrs. Eicher passed by."

"Did he identify Zimmer as the driver?"

"That's the thing. He's seen the assistant foreman on the building site, but Zimmer wasn't driving the truck. Another man was. An older guy. Early fifties, who sometimes hauls gravel for Castle."

"Are you saying Zimmer isn't the killer?"

"I'm saying there could be someone else we need to find. Be careful."

Noah disconnected and prayed again—the prayer he had continued to say since he had left the hospital.

"Protect Ruthie, Lord, and keep her safe."

Noah was worried. He had to find Ruthie. He had to find her now.

TWENTY-SIX

Ruthie struggled against the ropes around her hands and waist that held her bound to a kitchen chair. Her uncle had gone back to his car. The storm had grown worse, and she knew the water had to be rising higher. Her only hope was to free herself and escape while he was outside.

Using all her energy, she scooted the chair back toward the cabinet where she kept her cooking utensils. If only she could open the drawer, grab one of the knives and cut the ropes.

Between the booms of thunder, she listened for footsteps on the porch, then shoved the chair back again and again. Her legs ached with the effort. She glanced over her shoulder. A little farther and she would be near enough to try to open the drawer. If only she could.

Again, she inched the chair back, seeing the scratches it made on the floor. Nothing mattered except getting free. As unstable as her uncle acted, she knew he would never let her go.

She scooted back again. The chair was close. She raised her arms, tied behind her, and grasped the knob on the drawer, then tried to pull it open. She groaned. The chair was too close.

She inched the chair away from the counter, then raised her hands again. This time the drawer opened.

Pulling in a lungful of air, she stretched her arms even

higher to grab one of the knives. Her fingers latched onto a handle. She lifted it out only to have it drop to the floor.

Discouraged, she glanced down. A spoon. Not what she needed.

She tried again, and a wave of euphoria swept over her as her fingers touched the sharp blade of a knife. She almost cried with relief when she pulled it free.

Working quickly, she turned the knife in her hands and rubbed the blade against the rope with a back-and-forth motion.

The blade nicked her finger. She gasped and repositioned it. The rope was thick and the knife dull, but she continued trying.

Outside, the storm bellowed. Lightning illuminated the darkness.

Footsteps sounded on the porch.

Frantically, she hacked at the rope.

The door opened. Her uncle stepped inside, carrying a briefcase, and glanced at her. His faced twisted. "What are you doing?"

"Nothing." She tucked the knife against her arm.

He grabbed the chair and turned her around.

"Aren't you clever?" He jerked the knife from her hand. The blade scraped her wrist.

"Where is Andrew?" she demanded.

"If you obey me, he won't be hurt."

"Is he here at the farm? The river is rising. Do you have him in one of the outbuildings?"

He opened his briefcase and removed a stack of papers. "I'm going to untie your hands, but if you try anything, I won't let Andrew go."

"Please," she said, "he is a little boy. Do not hurt him."

Henry pulled the kitchen table closer to Ruthie and

untied her hands. She rubbed her wrists, feeling the circulation return.

He shoved a pen into her right hand and pointed to a line on the first paper.

"Sign your name here. The land goes to me because of your father's will. He placed the will in a safe deposit box at one of the banks. In case he was lying, I'll still have these signed forms deeding the farm to me."

"I do not know if my hand will work."

"Don't play games with me."

She took the pen and signed her name.

He turned to another page. "Sign here."

He pointed to another page, and another.

She dutifully signed on each line.

"Now let me know where you have taken Andrew. If anything has happened to him—"

She could not finish her sentence. The thought of her son being hurt cut into her heart.

Her uncle retied her hands behind her back and returned the signed papers to his briefcase.

"You're a fool, Ruthie, just like Ben said."

"You knew my husband?"

"What a waste of a man. He wasn't even a good poker player. He regretted marrying you, but he needed someplace to live. His family had kicked him out. You were an easy mark for him."

She did not care what he said about Ben and the way he had felt about her. There had been no love between them, though she had tried to be a dutiful wife. Somehow she had thought he had loved her in the beginning, though everything had changed too quickly.

"Tell me about Andrew," she pleaded.

The guy laughed. "Again, you're such a fool and so very gullible. I don't have Andrew. I tried to grab Simon in the hospital, but the nurses were always around so I followed you when you left town."

Relief swept over her and tears burned her eyes. Andrew must still be with Aunt Mattie, safe and protected.

"You tricked me," she said, "into signing the papers."

"I have your signature and that's all I need. Everyone will be upset about your passing."

"What?"

He glanced out the window. "The river is rising. The weather forecast is for continual rain for the next twelve hours. The water will enter the house soon."

Terror filled her, but she would not let him fool her again. She thought back to the flood when she was a girl. The water had come to the top of the kitchen counter. She glanced at that counter now, knowing her head would remain above water. Someone would eventually come to look for her. How long she could survive, she did not know, but she would not drown.

She wanted to rail against the man, yet she needed to placate him and play into his pity.

"Let me go. I will not say anything about you. I will not tell anyone that you forced me to sign the papers."

"Once again you are proving your foolishness. You would get that boyfriend of yours and run straight to the sheriff."

"I would not. I will talk Noah into signing over his property to you."

"That would be an added plus, but I realized I don't need his land. By shoring up the river on your side, the water will naturally form its own channel down the northern valley. I have gravel ready and sand to dam up the southern shore."

"The river is racing too quickly. You will never succeed, not when the water is this high."

"I worked on a dam in Chattanooga and know how to make it work."

She glanced at the cabinet. As soon as her uncle left, she would scoot the chair back again and get another knife from the drawer. This time she would be successful and cut through the rope.

"What are you thinking?" He stepped closer and saw the drawer. He pulled it open, then dumped the knives onto the counter and pushed them back toward the wall, too far for her to reach with her hands tied behind her back.

"And just in case you could get to the knives, I'll make sure you don't last long enough to try to free yourself."

Fear raced along her spine.

He grabbed the back of the chair and flipped it on its side.

Her head hit the floor, and she cried out in pain.

"I'll come back to remove the ropes after you're dead so no one will suspect foul play."

"Someone will see the marks on my wrists. They will know my death was not accidental. They will find you, Henry, and try you for murder."

He grabbed the briefcase and turned to gaze at her. "Your body will be bloated by the time they discover you, Ruthie. No one will look for marks on your wrists. Besides, I'm already a murderer."

"Please," she said.

He laughed, then hurried outside, slamming the door behind him.

Thunder rumbled overhead and another downpour of rain rattled against the tin roof.

Ruthie did not have long before the water would enter the house. She could raise her head a few inches off the floor, but once the water rose that high, she would not survive.

At least Andrew and Simon were safe. She loved them dearly. And Noah? She loved him, as well.

Noah turned off the mountain road and headed to Mattie's house. His heart was in his throat knowing something was wrong. Ruthie wouldn't have stayed away from the hospital this long no matter how bad the storm was.

The rain was blinding. Lightning zigzagged across the sky as if the storm was waging war against the earth.

He kept his eyes peeled as he drove, looking for signs that the buggy might have gone off the road. He crossed over a culvert that was swollen with rainwater.

His gut tightened—he feared Ruthie could have been caught in the rapid current.

The drive along the back road seemed to take forever. Every time he increased his speed, the vehicle would hydroplane. The pickup skidded twice. He eased up on the accelerator until he couldn't stand it any longer and then increased his speed again. He needed to find Ruthie as soon as possible and ensure she was all right.

He came around the final curve in the road and saw her aunt's house in the distance. After turning into the drive, he slammed on the brakes, leaped out of the truck and raced to the porch.

Aunt Mattie's eyes were wide when she opened the door. "Has something happened to Simon?"

Noah shook his head. "He's improving. I need to talk to Ruthie."

"Ruthie is not here. I thought she was at the hospital with you."

Noah's chest compressed and he exhaled a lungful of air. "She didn't stop here to check on Andrew?"

The boy ran to the door. "Noah, where's *Mamm*? And how is Simon?"

"Your brother is better." He didn't want to worry Andrew, but he needed to speak truthfully to Mattie.

She understood his hesitation. "Andrew, go get the cake I cut today. Noah can take it to the hospital for your brother and mother."

Once the boy raced into the kitchen, Mattie grabbed Noah's hand. "How long ago did Ruthie leave the hospital?"

"Long enough for her to have gotten here, had cake and returned." He raked his hand through his hair and turned to glance at the dark sky and torrential rain. "Where is she, Mattie?"

"I do not know."

Noah couldn't wait any longer. He raced to his truck and guided it back onto the road. Glancing in his rearview mirror, he saw Andrew on the porch holding a tin that, no doubt, held the cake. Much as he hated to disappoint the young boy, Noah had no time to waste. Ruthie was in danger. Had the man found her, and if so, where would he take her? Law enforcement was looking for him in town. The only place left was the mountain.

He reached for his cell and called the sheriff's department. The phone went to voice mail. With the bad weather, there was no telling where the deputies were needed. He envisioned accidents on the main road, perhaps flooding in the southern valley, downed power lines and people caught in the storm.

"This is Noah Schlabach. Ruthie Eicher is missing. I fear the man who attacked her has kidnapped her. I don't have any information, but do whatever you can to find her. I'm heading up the mountain to her property if the river hasn't already overflowed its banks. I'll try to keep you posted, but cell reception isn't good and the storm doesn't help."

He disconnected and threw the phone onto the console.

Needing an update on the rising river, he flipped on the radio. Static buzzed, followed by the announcer's voice.

"The main mountain road is flooded. Take the northern route if you're heading up Amish Mountain."

Noah's heart sank. The detour would take more time. Time he didn't have. Yet his instincts screamed that he had to get to Ruthie's farm.

He angled across one of the side roads and crossed the lower bridge to the northern shore that would lead to his father's property. He hoped the bridge connecting his farm to Ruthie's would still be standing.

Water covered the road, but he continued to drive at a rapid speed. Noah didn't care what happened to him, but he had to find Ruthie. Her life was in danger—he knew that for sure.

He had to find her before the terrible man who had attacked her turned on her again. This time the man on the mountain wouldn't be satisfied with striking Ruthie and kicking her. This time he would kill her.

TWENTY-SEVEN

Ruthie glanced at the woodstove and spotted the poker. Would the metal tip be sharp enough to cut through the rope?

She jerked back on the chair and inched her way toward the stove. Her cheek rubbed against the floor. She fisted her hands to counter the pain and kept moving the chair little by little. Her progress was slow, but anything was better than doing nothing. If there was hope, she would continue to fight for her life.

Water flowed under the front door and fanned out on the hardwood floors. A braided rug soaked up some of the moisture. A second surge of water flowed in, circled the rug and headed toward where she was lying. She pushed herself back again and again, nearing the stove as the water inched toward her. Another wave of water traveled across the main room and splashed against her arm.

Her heart nearly stopped.

She pushed again, then reached for the poker. It slipped from her hands and dropped to the floor behind her, knocking against her head.

As much as she wanted to cry, she would not sacrifice her precious energy when she was fighting for her life.

Again, she scooted the chair and repositioned her hands closer to the metal rod.

Another surge of water flowed around her ear.

She stretched her arms behind her and flailed her fingers, searching for the poker.

Her hands touched something hard and circular. She grabbed the metal rod, overcome with relief. Slowly she inched her fingers along the poker until she felt the blunt tip.

Blunt?

She shoved the rod against the rope, holding her bound hands, but without a sharp end, her efforts were for naught.

She closed her eyes. *Please,* Gott, *save me.*

When she opened her eyes, another wave of water streamed across the floor and splashed against her cheek. In a short time, the water would rise higher and cover her nose and her mouth.

Ruthie could not think of that now. She had to get free. But how?

Amish Mountain was barely visible with the low cloud cover and blinding rain. Noah gripped the wheel with white knuckles and forced his truck up the hill. The rain-soaked earth couldn't absorb any more moisture, so water covered the road.

Mudslides could be a problem. *Please,* Gott, *don't let that happen. I have enough worries trying to find Ruthie.*

The storm raged outside the truck and sounded like a monster attacking the earth.

Lightning brightened the sky, creating an eerie hue that flashed on and off.

The engine sputtered going around a curve. He eased his foot off the gas pedal. "Come on. Don't give out on me now."

Nearing the final turn, he held his breath and rounded the bend. His father's farmhouse and the bridge were still standing. In spite of the raging river, both structures remained intact. He spied a car parked on the distant shore.

"Stay with me, Lord," he prayed as he coaxed his truck over the rickety bridge that swayed in the storm. Water washed over the underpinnings and sloshed against the wheels of his pickup.

"Don't let the engine stall," he said aloud.

Once across the river, he parked on higher ground, then leaped from his truck. Thunder crashed overhead and rain pummeled him. For half a heartbeat, the storm ebbed before the next clap of thunder rumbled across the sky. In that momentary lull, Noah heard another sound—the sound of a loud engine.

He followed the noise around the back of the barn and down to the river. The rapid current was flowing at breakneck speed and the water had flooded over the riverbank.

The rain eased for a moment, and he saw a bulldozer pushing soil and debris into the water, forming a man-made dam. A dump truck sat parked nearby. Gravel sprayed across the side of the riverbed.

A guy dressed in black operated the bulldozer. The angry current tried to tear apart his work, but he backed up again and shoved an even larger mix of gravel and soil into the river.

Surely the man wasn't in his right mind to be operating heavy equipment at the edge of a flooding river, and no telling how he had gotten the bulldozer and dump truck up the mountain. Noah glanced around to ensure he didn't have an accomplice or two hiding in the bushes.

From what Noah could tell, the man was working alone, and he was making progress. Water spilled over the opposite bank of the river and washed down the mountain, along the northern valley Noah and Ruthie had seen when they'd toured Castle Homes.

Ruthie had been right. The guy wanted her land so he could detour the water and form a new river that would feed into Castle's lake.

Noah raced forward. The man backed up the bulldozer, nearly running over Noah.

He grabbed the man's arm and yanked him from the seat. The guy swung his fist and hit Noah in the chin.

Ignoring the pain, he grabbed the man's arm again.

"Where is she?" Noah screamed above the roar of the storm. "What did you do with Ruthie?"

"Get outta my way. This is my land now."

Noah jabbed his fists into the guy's stomach. The man doubled over, coughing and gasping for air.

"Where is she?" Noah grabbed his shoulders and held him up. "Where's Ruthie?"

"I told you this land is mine. You're trespassing."

The guy struggled to free himself. Noah wrapped his hands around his chest and half dragged, half pushed him toward the barn. Using electrical tape from the tool rack, he bound his hands and feet, then dragged him to his pickup and hoisted him into the bed of the truck.

The guy groaned.

Noah grabbed his shirt and leaned into his face. "You've got one more chance. Where is she?"

The guy nervously flicked his gaze toward the Plank house.

"She's in there?" Noah shoved him aside and raced to the house. The river had already flooded over the porch.

"Ruthie?" Noah pushed open the door. All he could see was the rising water.

He called her name again. Movement by the woodstove alerted him. An overturned chair.

His pulse raced. Ruthie was tied to the chair, with her

nose and mouth underwater. At that instant, she raised up her head and grabbed a breath.

Heart in his throat, he ran to her, lifted her out of the water and righted the chair that still held her bound.

"Oh, Ruthie!" He found a knife on the nearby counter and cut through the ropes. All the while, she gasped for air, then coughed and sputtered.

"I tied up the guy who attacked you, but I didn't think I would find you in time." He looked into her eyes. "Talk to me. Are you okay?"

She rubbed her hands together and then patted her chest and coughed.

More water swept into the house.

"We need to get out of here now." Noah lifted her into his arms and carried her across the room, through the water and out the door. The rain pelted them, but he had Ruthie and he wouldn't let her go.

TWENTY-EIGHT

Ruthie collapsed onto the seat of Noah's pickup. She was shaken to the core and kept thinking of what could have happened if Noah had not saved her. Overcome with emotion, she dropped her head in her hands and started to cry.

He climbed behind the wheel and pulled her into his arms. She nestled closer as the tears fell.

"Shhh," he soothed, rubbing her back and giving her time to regain her composure.

Warmed by his embrace and drawing strength from him, she eventually wiped her hands over her face. "You saved me, Noah. I am so grateful, but I am also wet and dirty."

He smiled. "You're beautiful and you're alive, but we need to get out of here before the water rises any higher."

He started the engine and turned onto the road heading up the mountain. "There's a narrow roadway that weaves around the back of Amish Mountain. It will take us longer to get to town, but it's far from the river. I'm driving directly to the hospital so the doctors can examine you. No telling what you were exposed to in the water."

"I need to see the boys."

"Andrew is fine. He's with Mattie. Simon's fever is down and he was feeling better when I left the hospital."

"The man who tried to kill me was my uncle Henry. He said he had Andrew and would harm him if I did not turn over my land to him. I signed the papers he provided in order to save my son."

"Both boys are being cared for, and we'll determine if the papers you signed are legal later." He wrapped a blanket over her, and she pulled it close.

"You saved me in the nick of time, Noah. I could not have lasted a second longer. The water kept rising, and…" She paused for a long moment. "I…I did not think I would survive."

"And I didn't think I would ever find you."

"My uncle stopped me on the way to my aunt's house and forced me into the trunk of his car. He hid the buggy in the woods. I am sure Buttercup is frightened to death by now."

"We'll get her. I looked for you when I drove to Mattie's farm, fearing I would find the buggy crashed on the side of the road."

"Which was almost the case. Where is Henry now?"

"In the back of my truck."

"What?" Glancing through the rear window, she saw her uncle and sighed, overcome with regret that her own kin had tried to kill her.

"Henry needed to get rid of me so he could have the farm." She explained about her father's will that supposedly gave her uncle rights to the land if she ever left the property. "The foreman planned to buy the property from him, then changed his mind. Uncle Henry killed him and tried to kill me."

Noah rubbed her shoulder. "It's over, Ruthie."

"*Yah*, but I will feel better once I know the boys are all right."

"We'll get to the hospital as soon as possible."

"Did you talk to the real-estate agent about your land?" she asked.

He nodded.

Ruthie's heart sunk. Why had she thought Noah might change his mind?

The flashing lights of the deputy sheriff's squad car appeared on the road ahead. Noah pulled up beside the car and rolled down his window, obviously happy to see Deputy Warren.

"I got your voice mail, Noah. Looks like you didn't need me."

Noah explained what had happened and then pointed his thumb to the rear of the truck. "I've got the man who attacked Ruthie tied up in the rear. Arrest him, Deputy, for the murder of Brian Burkholder, as well as the attempted murder of Ruthie Eicher."

The deputy looked at Ruthie. "Did he hurt you, ma'am?"

"He tied me up and left me in my flooded home to drown, but Noah saved me."

The deputy stepped from his car and slapped Noah's shoulder. "You're a good man, Noah Schlabach. We could use you around this neck of the woods if you decide to stay."

Noah squeezed Ruthie's hand before he stepped to the pavement and followed the deputy to the rear of his pickup. Ruthie slipped from the pickup and watched as he lowered the back of the truck bed. Noah grabbed the tape binding her uncle's legs, pulled him to the edge and then eased him to his feet.

"I'm innocent," Henry railed. "Noah Schlabach trespassed on my property," her uncle said to the deputy. "I've got the deed in my briefcase."

"And where's your briefcase?" the deputy asked.

"Probably floating down the river," Noah said as he

herded the guy toward the rear door of the squad car that Deputy Warren held open.

"We'll take you downtown and have a long talk. You can tell me about beating up a defenseless woman and leaving her to die in a flood."

Once Henry was secured in the rear of the squad car, the deputy addressed Ruthie. "Ma'am, I'll connect with you later and take your statement. Don't worry about this guy. He's staying behind bars."

Noah shook the deputy's hand and then helped Ruthie back into the pickup.

The deputy raced down the mountain, siren screaming and lights flashing as Noah climbed behind the wheel.

"We'll take it a bit slower," he said with a smile.

"Just so we get to the hospital so I can see Simon."

"We're heading there now."

People stared at Ruthie's wet and muddy clothing when she got to the hospital, but she did not care. All she wanted was to see Simon and ensure her son was all right.

When she stepped into his room, her heart nearly burst with relief. Not only was Simon sitting up in bed looking bright-eyed and energetic, but Andrew and Aunt Mattie were also there. The boys were playing checkers while Mattie sat knitting in a nearby chair.

Andrew spied her first. *"Mamm,"* he shouted. Hopping off the bed, he raced with open arms to hug her.

"Oh, Andrew, it is so good to see you."

She gave him a hug and, still holding his hand, hurried to the bed and hugged Simon with her other arm. "You are cool. Your fever is gone."

"And I feel strong, *Mamm*. The nurse said I can go home tomorrow."

Home? She worried where that would be with the flooded house on Amish Mountain.

"We were worried about you," Mattie said as she placed her knitting on a bedside table and hurried to embrace Ruthie.

"I am a mess."

"You look wonderful. One of the Amish farmers who lives near me spotted your buggy and mare. Both are safe in my barn. After that, Andrew and I called the Amish taxi and rode here in his car. We were worried. Simon and Andrew suggested we pray together, which is what we did. The boys knew that *Gott* would answer their prayers."

Ruthie smiled with maternal pride and gratitude for her two sons. "*Gott* did answer your prayers, boys. He brought Noah, who saved me from that hateful man. The sheriff has him locked up now, so we no longer have to worry."

"What about the farm, *Mamm*?" Simon asked. "Are we staying or leaving?"

"We are staying, Simon. Although we will have to work hard to clean the house after the flooding."

Simon looked at Noah, his gaze intense. "What about you? Are you staying or leaving?"

Ruthie was not ready for the boys to learn that Noah was leaving. She needed to prepare them a bit before she gave them the news. They would be so disappointed, and she did not want this moment of reunion to be ruined with more upset.

"Perhaps Noah will tell us at a later time."

"No, Ruthie, I can tell you now."

"I do not think that is wise. Simon is just starting to improve, and we are all tired and have been through so much."

"Which is the perfect time to tell you that I'm staying."

"What?"

"Yay!" the boys cheered in unison. Andrew grabbed

Noah around the waist and Simon slipped from bed and hugged him, as well.

"Simon, get back in bed," Ruthie insisted.

She felt light-headed and unsure she had heard Noah correctly. "You are not selling your land?"

"That's correct. I'm staying on Amish Mountain. It's my home. I have wonderful neighbors and an Amish community that I never should have left."

"But—"

"I made a mistake years ago, Ruthie. I left you and I left my heart with you. I've tried to make a life for myself, but I was going through the motions when all along I wanted to be back here with you."

He glanced at the boys. "And with Simon and Andrew, these wonderful young men who have also stolen my heart."

Ruthie was confused and unable to share in the boys' excitement. Had Noah been away from the Amish faith so long he did not realize that which would continue to separate them?

"Is there a problem, Ruthie?" he asked, no doubt seeing her concern.

Why did he not realize they could never be together when...?

"You—you are *Englisch*, Noah," she blurted out.

He smiled. "Not for long. I plan to talk to the bishop as soon as possible."

Had she heard him correctly? "Are you sure this is what you want to do?"

"I've never been surer about anything. As long as you don't mind me staying. I know you're still grieving and—"

She gripped his arm and stepped closer. "I grieved for you when you left. We must have exchanged hearts because you took mine with you."

"You're sure?"

"Cross my heart." She laughed as tears of joy flowed down her cheeks.

"I never thought you would want me back, Ruthie, so I never came home."

"We both made mistakes, but that is in the past, and what is important is the present." She looked at the boys. "And the future."

"A future together, Ruthie."

She nodded and rested her head on Noah's shoulder as they both smiled at Simon and Andrew. "Yes, dear Noah, a future where we are all together."

The nurse knocked and entered the room. "Looks like everyone's been out in the storm."

Ruthie explained to the nurse some of what happened.

"The doctor is at the nurses' station. Let's have him check you over. He might want to run some tests."

Before Ruthie left the room, Mattie had Noah call the Amish taxi for her. "Andrew and I will go home and prepare the house. I want all of you to stay with me until the flooding ends and your homes are ready to be lived in again."

"That is so generous," Ruthie said.

"We are family, Ruth Ann. Family takes care of its own. We have been separated too long. We will not let that happen again."

Ruthie hugged her aunt.

"I will ask the taxi driver to return to the hospital with clean clothes for you to wear," Mattie said. "We are about the same size. I even have a new *kapp* that should fit you. I am certain the nurse will let you shower here. I doubt she wants the river mud in her hospital room."

"Thank you, Mattie. We will see you tomorrow."

After Mattie and Andrew left, Ruthie headed for the

nurses' station. The doctor prescribed an antibiotic due to the water she had swallowed. "If you start feeling sick, I'll want to see you again."

"What about our well situation?"

"I doubt your well water was the problem, Mrs. Eicher, since your younger son didn't get sick, but you'll need to have it tested after this flooding."

Ruthie told him about the two milk jugs and her concern that Henry had contaminated one of the jugs.

The doctor rubbed his jaw and nodded. "That would certainly explain why only one of your sons became ill. If not for the flood, we could culture the jugs, although I'm sure they're long gone by now. I'm just glad you brought Simon to the ER in time. We'll keep him on oral meds for the next ten days. If he shows any signs of reoccurring infection, you'll need to bring him back."

"Thank you for taking care of my son."

"He's a good boy. I hope we'll see more of you and your family in town."

"*Yah*, we will come often, I am certain."

Later, once she had showered and changed into the clothing Mattie sent, Ruthie started to relax. The deputy stopped by and had her write up what had happened and then sign her statement.

"Don't worry," Deputy Warren assured her. "Henry Plank won't get out on bail. He'll stay behind bars, and I feel sure the jury, when he goes to trial, won't have any problem with their verdict. You'll have to testify, ma'am, but he confessed to killing Brian Burkholder and attacking you. He also said he had tainted some milk left outside at your house."

The deputy glanced at Simon. "That might be what caused your boy to get sick."

Ruthie was relieved that the well water had not been

the problem and thankful for the doctor and medical staff at the hospital.

"Mr. Plank said you had signed papers he had downloaded off his computer that deeded the land to him. We talked to one of the county lawyers who assured us the forms you signed, if they ever turn up after that flood, would not be legally binding."

"I am relieved," Ruthie said, "and I appreciate you checking with a lawyer."

"Happy to help, ma'am."

The deputy glanced out the window. "I doubt you folks have heard what happened. That dam the guy managed to put in place detoured a good bit of water into that northern valley, which means the south side of town suffered no flooding."

"So his plan had positive results."

"The townspeople who didn't get their shops flooded feel that way, although the construction in the Castle Homes area has a problem."

"What happened?" Noah asked.

"Water washed out some of their new construction. A number of folks who planned to purchase homes have changed their minds. The Atlanta paper published an online story about the foreman's death and people are calling to say they're not interested in buying a Castle home."

The deputy held up his hand. "There's more. The bank said if Castle can't make this month's mortgage payment, his land will go to foreclosure."

"Castle will lose everything?" Ruthie asked.

"Yes, ma'am. He's talking about a development in Mississippi that he plans to tackle next."

"He's always trying to make it rich," Noah said.

The deputy nodded in agreement. "Money and power

are important to Mr. Castle. That is a shame. He needs to learn the importance of truth and service to others."

Deputy Warren paused for a moment and then added, "There's an interesting side story that the Atlanta reporter uncovered. Brian Burkholder's son, Prescott, lived in Mr. Castle's Chattanooga development that flooded. Seems Prescott saved a lot of folks' lives that night, including children who couldn't swim and wouldn't have survived without him. He went back to get a young family with a little girl named Mary, but he didn't make it. They all perished, but the young man was a hero for sure. That's why Burkholder named the company after his son. He planned to use any profits he earned from Castle to help the survivors of that flood."

"By any chance, do you know the name of the family Prescott tried to save?" Noah asked.

"Seth was the man's first name." The deputy rubbed his jaw. "Give me a minute and I'll remember the last name."

Ruthie looked at Noah's expectant gaze and reached for his hand.

The deputy nodded. "Seth Schlabach." His eyes widened as he glanced at Noah. "Any relation?"

Stepping closer, Ruthie wrapped her arm around Noah's waist. She could sense the lump in his throat when he spoke.

"Seth Schlabach was my brother."

The deputy patted Noah's shoulder. "I'm sorry for your loss."

"It helps to know that someone tried to save them."

"Just like you saved me," Ruthie said.

Deputy Warren stood quietly for a long moment and she knew he had been touched, as well.

Finally, he said, "I talked to some of the local townspeople, Mrs. Eicher. They want to help clean up your property."

"I—I never thought they cared, although the bishop and some of the women stopped by the farm a few times, usually when Ben was in town gambling. I refused to see them. It was my hurt pride after the church had shunned my husband. I understood why it happened, but my heart remained closed to their outreach even after Ben died."

The deputy nodded. "Folks feel real bad about you having to manage the farm by yourself. I talked to the bishop. He plans to visit you soon. The district will pay for Simon's hospital bills."

Tears burned Ruthie's eyes.

"The bishop said he hopes you'll come back to Sunday services."

She smiled and looked at Simon. "That would be *gut*."

"I need to talk to him, as well," Noah said.

"You all are staying in town for the next few days?"

"My aunt Mattie has room for us. You can find us there."

The deputy smiled. "I'll let the bishop know."

Noah and Ruthie walked the deputy to the elevator and said goodbye to him there.

A small waiting room was across the hall. Noah took Ruthie's hand and guided her into the room, then pulled the door closed behind them.

"I wanted to talk to you in private, Ruthie."

"What is it?" she asked, suddenly worried. "Have you changed your mind about staying?"

"No. I'm here for good. But I wanted to ask you something and perhaps it's too soon with Ben gone such a short time."

"What is it, Noah?" She was even more concerned.

"Ruthie, I've loved you forever. I told you that earlier,

and it's true. You've always had my heart. Coming back, I realized how foolish I had been, how stupid. I had everything, and I left it here so that I could make my own way because of my father and my lack of understanding. I wasn't man enough to forgive him, so I caused you and Simon so much pain."

"It is over, Noah."

"No, Ruthie. I don't want it to be over. I want it to be the beginning of us together. You and the boys and me. I'm not doing this very well because I'm not sure what you will say and that has me tongue-tied."

He hesitated and then took her hands and stared into her eyes. "Ruthie, will you forgive me and let me make it up to you? I want to marry you when you have time to sort through everything that has happened. I love both your boys as my own and promise to be the best father I can be to Simon and Andrew. Will you give me a second chance?"

He hesitated for a moment and then added, "Will you marry me?"

"Oh, Noah, you do not need a second chance. You have always had my heart. I have never stopped loving you. Yes, I will marry you. Nothing would make me happier and I know the boys will be overjoyed, too."

"We don't have to rush into anything. I'll need to be baptized first."

"We have waited so long. Your baptism cannot come soon enough."

He pulled her close and lowered his lips to hers, and everything she had ever wanted in life came to fruition in that one kiss. The promise of a future together, of more children, of a new home on the mountain and a wonderful life with Noah as her husband.

"I have never loved anyone else," she whispered as he kissed her again and again.

Eventually, she pulled back and giggled like a school-girl. "Simon will wonder what happened to us."

"He'll know something's going on by the way you're blushing."

"And you." She laughed. "You have the biggest smile I have ever seen."

"That's because you've made me the happiest man in the world."

Arm in arm, they walked back to Simon's room, to see their son. Tomorrow at Mattie's house they would tell both boys about Noah's desire to return to the Amish faith and their upcoming marriage. When the boys were older, they would tell them who Simon's father really was. Ruthie felt certain the information would be well received.

As they stepped into Simon's room, Ruthie glanced out the window. The rain had stopped and the sun was shining. In the distant sky, she saw the most beautiful rainbow as a sign from *Gott* that the storm had ended and the future would be bright and filled with love.

EPILOGUE

"Hurry, boys," Noah called to Simon and Andrew. They both ran from the house wearing their new straw hats and athletic shoes. Andrew stopped on the porch to tie his laces, then hopped down the stairs and raced to the buggy.

"I can run so fast now." His smile was wide and his eyes bright.

"Race you to Aunt Mattie's mailbox and back," Simon challenged.

Noah laughed as he watched the boys run. Andrew won but only because Simon slowed so his younger brother could pass by him.

Returning to the buggy, Simon winked at Noah, who winked back.

"Andrew's growing so fast," Noah said to Simon. "Soon he will be as tall as you."

Andrew stood on tiptoe and came up to Simon's chin.

"Yah." Simon joined in the fun. "He is tall like a weed."

"I am tall like a sweetgum tree," the younger boy countered.

"Then you produce spiky seed pods that cause pain when I step on them," Simon added.

Andrew shook his head. "Not with our new shoes. We do not have to worry where we step now."

"As long as you remember to wear your rubber boots when there is mud," Noah cautioned.

"Like after the flood?"

"*Yah*." Noah nodded. "You were *gut* workers as we swept the mud from the old house."

"*Mamm* said it still smells."

"That's why we're building the new house."

"Where we will live after your wedding."

"*Yah*, Andrew." Noah patted the boy's shoulder. "That's right. A new home for our new family."

Simon rubbed Buttercup's mane. "Andrew and I were talking about the wedding when we went to bed last night."

"Oh?" Noah would have enjoyed hearing that conversation.

Andrew stepped closer. "We are both glad you are going to be our new *datt*."

Noah's heart warmed. "Thank you, boys. I'm glad, as well."

"But," Simon added, "it does not seem that you are a new *datt*."

"Meaning what?" Noah asked, confused by the boy's comment.

"Meaning it seems that you are our *datt*. Not a new one, but the one who we have waited for all our lives."

Noah wanted to say something about Ben being a *gut datt*, but he was overcome with gratitude and did not want to change anything about the moment as he gazed at his son.

"You have always been in my heart, Simon." He glanced at Andrew. "And you, as well, Andrew. So thank you for allowing me to have a place in your family. Thank you for allowing me to be your *datt*."

He opened his arms and the boys stepped into his embrace. Noah's heart soared with joy for these two sons of his. He had asked *Gott* to forgive him for leaving Ruthie so long ago. She had endured so much. The boys had, too. Now they were together as a family, which was more than Noah deserved and more than he had ever expected, but then Ruthie had assured him that *Gott* was a generous provider.

Ruthie stepped from the kitchen, carrying a basket filled with their picnic lunch. Simon ran to help her and placed the basket carefully in the rear of the buggy.

"Climb in, boys." Noah motioned them into the buggy. "Let's go to our new house and enjoy the lunch your *mamm* prepared for us."

Aunt Mattie came onto the porch and waved. "Remember the bishop is coming for dinner this evening."

"We'll be home in plenty of time," Noah promised as he flicked the reins and encouraged Buttercup up Amish Mountain.

The sun was bright and the air smelled sweetly of honeysuckle.

"It will be *gut* to move back to the mountain after the house is finished," Simon said.

Noah reached for Ruthie's hand. "Remember, Simon, home is anywhere as long as we're together."

Ruthie's eyes beamed and her skin glowed. The lines of worry and concern that had weighed her down were gone, replaced with an infectious joy that he remembered from their youth.

The boys sang as they rode up the mountain, their voices harmonizing. Ruthie and Noah joined in, and between the songs, they laughed and joked.

Turning onto the farm, they passed the old house and headed to the new one, positioned higher on the rise and away from the river. Even if it flooded again, the water wouldn't come into their new home.

The boys hopped down and raced along the meadow,

chasing butterflies and enjoying the fresh air and the open spaces.

Noah pulled Ruthie close and pointed to the valley. "Castle Homes is gone and the area will soon bear new growth as the trees return."

"It is like a distant memory that I do not want to recall." She squeezed his hand. "All I want to think about is our wedding and our future together."

"The boys told me they're glad I will be their new *datt*, then added that it seemed they had been waiting for me all along. I should have corrected them, but my heart was overflowing with love for both of them and I didn't want to spoil the moment."

"I told you, Noah, you have always been in my heart. They knew you because I carried you within me. My love for you never ended, and even the years when we were apart, you were with me."

"You led me back to the mountain, Ruthie, and back to the Amish faith. I thank *Gott* for that."

"You returned when I needed you most. You saved us from my uncle. I might have left my land, and look what I would have lost."

They stared at the valley that stretched below and the gentle river that flowed between their properties.

"The new bridge looks sturdy," Ruthie said. "You did a *gut* job rebuilding it."

"The underpinnings survived the flood, and the bridge stayed intact long enough for me to save you. My father built that bridge soon after he and my mother married. I have been remembering those happy times when Seth and I were children."

"You have forgiven your *datt*?"

"*Yah*, and that forgiveness has healed the wound within me that festered for so long."

Ruthie smiled. "I found my father's will along with a note he wrote to me explaining that he knew you and I were meant to be together, but he also knew the farm needed to stay within the family. Henry had convinced my father that he wanted to reconcile and be part of the family again so my *datt* arranged for the farm to go to him if I moved away from the mountain."

"Your *datt* loved you, Ruthie."

She nodded. "In his own way, he did love me."

"Now, with my father's land and your father's land joined together, we will have a flourishing farm."

"You will teach the boys to be *gut* farmers."

Noah wrapped his arm more tightly around her waist. "There will be much to do, but they are hard workers, like their mother."

She smiled and scooted closer.

"I am glad the new house will be ready before the wedding," he said. "Your aunt Mattie told me the boys can stay with her for a few days following the service so we can enjoy our new home together."

"What do you plan to do when we're alone?" Ruthie asked.

"Tell you how much I love you and have always loved you. I want to share every moment of every day with you, Ruthie. Together we'll farm the land and help our boys grow into wonderful men."

"And other children?" she asked, her eyes twinkling.

"That's something I'm planning for. Little girls who look like you and boys who look like Simon. We can add on to the house, if need be. I also want to renovate my father's home. It's rundown and needs work, but someday Simon might want to live there."

Ruthie nodded. "With his wife and children."

"Our grandchildren." Noah smiled. "We have a wonderful life ahead of us."

She snuggled deeper into his embrace. "The future sounds better than I ever could have imagined, Noah."

"I love you, Ruthie. I've always loved you. Thank you for forgiving me and inviting me back into your life."

She shook her head. "Noah, I told you. You have always been with me. I never said goodbye, because deep down in my heart I knew you would come back to me."

She raised her lips to his. "And you did."

* * * * *

Dear Reader,

I hope you enjoyed this second-chance-at-love story. Ten years ago, Noah Schlabach left Amish Mountain and the woman he loved, never knowing she was pregnant with his son. Returning home, he finds Ruthie Eicher widowed and trying to care for her two boys, as well as maintain their farm. But someone is out to do her harm, and Noah will do anything to keep her and the boys safe.

I pray for my readers each day and would love to hear from you. Email me at debby@debbygiusti.com, write me c/o Love Inspired, 195 Broadway, 24th Floor, New York, NY 10007 or visit me at www.DebbyGiusti.com and at www.facebook.com/debby.giusti.9.

As always, I thank God for bringing us together through this story.

Wishing you abundant blessings,
Debby